D1135128

ALSO BY
STUART GIBBS

THE FUNJUNGLE
SERIES

Belly Up

Poached

Big Game

Panda-monium

Lion Down

Tyrannosaurus Wrecks

Bear Bottom

Whale Done

THE SPY SCHOOL
SERIES

Spy School

Spy Camp

Evil Spy School

Spy Ski School

Spy School Secret Service

Spy School Goes South

Spy School British Invasion

Spy School Revolution

Spy School at Sea

Spy School Project X

(with Anjan Sarkar)

Spy School the Graphic Novel

Spy Camp the Graphic Novel

THE MOON
BASE ALPHA SERIES

Space Case

Spaced Out

Waste of Space

THE CHARLIE
THORNE SERIES

*Charlie Thorne
and the Last Equation*

Charlie Thorne and the Lost City

*Charlie Thorne and
the Curse of Cleopatra*

THE ONCE UPON
A TIM SERIES

Once Upon a Tim

The Labyrinth of Doom

The Last Musketeer

THE SEA OF TERROR

ONCE UPON A TIM
BOOK 3

STUART GIBBS

ILLUSTRATED BY STACY CURTIS

SIMON & SCHUSTER BOOKS FOR YOUNG READERS
NEW YORK LONDON TORONTO SYDNEY NEW DELHI

SIMON & SCHUSTER BOOKS FOR YOUNG READERS

An imprint of Simon & Schuster Children's Publishing Division

1230 Avenue of the Americas, New York, New York 10020

SIMON & SCHUSTER BOOKS FOR YOUNG READERS

and related marks are trademarks of Simon & Schuster, Inc.

For information about special discounts for bulk purchases, please contact Simon & Schuster Special Sales at 1-866-506-1949 or business@simonandschuster.com.

The Simon & Schuster Speakers Bureau can bring authors to your live event. For more information or to book an event, contact the Simon & Schuster Speakers Bureau at 1-866-248-3049 or visit our website at www.simonspeakers.com.

Interior design by Tom Daly

The text for this book was set in Adobe Caslon Pro.

The illustrations for this book were rendered in pen and ink.

Manufactured in the United States of America

0323 FFG

First Edition

2 4 6 8 10 9 7 5 3 1

Library of Congress Cataloging-in-Publication Data

Names: Gibbs, Stuart, 1969– author. | Curtis, Stacy, illustrator.

Title: The sea of terror / Stuart Gibbs ; illustrated by Stacy Curtis.

Description: First edition. | New York : Simon & Schuster Books for Young Readers, [2023] | Series: Once upon a Tim ; 3 | Audience: Ages 7 to 10. | Audience: Grades 2-3. | Summary: Tim and his friends travel by land and sea, collecting treasure and defeating monsters as they go.

Identifiers: LCCN 2022000197 (print) | LCCN 2022000198 (ebook) | ISBN 9781665917445 | ISBN 9781665917469 (ebook)

Subjects: CYAC: Knights and knighthood—Fiction. | Adventure and adventurers—Fiction. | Humorous stories. | LCGFT: Humorous fiction. | Novels.

Classification: LCC PZ7.G339236 Se 2023 (print) | LCC PZ7.G339236 (ebook) | DDC [Fic]—dc23

LC record available at https://lccn.loc.gov/2022000197

LC ebook record available at https://lccn.loc.gov/2022000198

For Walker and Maxine

—S. G.

For Fred and Jeanne Borger

—S. C.

CHAPTER ONE

What I Was Afraid Of

ONCE UPON A TIME...

You could barely get through the day without running into a vicious, bloodthirsty creature.

The countryside was crawling with them. Literally.

And, as a member of the Knight Brigade of the Great and Glorious Kingdom of Merryland, it was my job to fend them off.

This was not easy.

In fact, it was extremely difficult. And potentially deadly. And scary. Just turn the page and you'll see what I mean.

I'm the knight on the left. My name is Tim. The other knight is my best friend, Belinda. And that big ugly thing we are facing is a bargleboar.

Now, I know what you're thinking. You're thinking, *Bargleboar? I've never heard of one of those. There's no such thing.*

Well, just because you haven't heard of something doesn't mean it didn't exist.

Back in olden times, there were *plenty* of vicious, bloodthirsty creatures you've probably never heard of: bargleboars, blugslugs, bungbears, bandersplatters, boombugs, bladebeasts, bloodmongers . . . and that's just the *b*s. I'll admit that, even in my day, they weren't well known. Because anyone who encountered one of them usually didn't live long enough to tell anyone else about it.

Here's something else you are probably thinking: *Gosh, Tim and Belinda don't look old enough to be knights.*

That is true. We were quite young. In fact, we were still knights-in-training.

Even though knights have to do extremely dangerous things like fight bargleboars, we had actually volunteered for the job. Because back in our time, there were only two job options for a boy: knight and peasant. (And as a girl, Belinda didn't even have the option of being a knight; she had pretended to be a boy to join up.) Being a peasant was *boring*. Do you like doing chores? Well, imagine doing chores from the moment you get up until the moment you go to bed, with only an occasional break for a bowl of gruel. That's what being a peasant was like.

Being a knight might have been dangerous, scary, and exhausting, but it was also very exciting. Belinda and I hadn't been on the Knight Brigade for very long, but we'd already had plenty of amazing adventures.

We weren't the *only* knights fighting the bargleboar, mind you. Several others were there with us, despite the danger.

Sir Cuss was always in a bad mood and eager to stab something. Sir Mount liked to look dashing astride his horse and impress the local maidens. Sir Cumference knew that whoever killed a bargleboar got first dibs on the best parts of the animal to eat. Sir Fass looked up to Sir Cuss and copied whatever he did. Sir Vaylance claimed his job was to oversee the battle, but I'm pretty

sure that was just a clever excuse to keep his distance.

Meanwhile, our leader, Sir Vyval, wasn't even at the battle at all. Instead, he was shouting orders from the ramparts of the castle, well out of the bargleboar's goring range. But then, one of the perks of being the leader of the knights was that you got to make everyone else do all the dangerous stuff.

"Stab it!" Sir Vyval yelled to us, as if perhaps none of us knew what our swords were for. "Stab it hard! Kill it!!!"

"You heard our fearless leader!" Sir Mount announced gallantly, nice and loud so that all the maidens could hear him. "Go kill that bargleboar!"

(It is worth noting that Sir Mount never personally followed Sir Vyval's orders. He only repeated them bravely to us without doing any of the dangerous bits. Also, it is much easier to be courageous when you are the only knight with a horse; if things go bad, you can escape faster than everyone else, leaving them all behind to be eaten.)

As the lowest-ranking members of the Knight Brigade, Belinda and I had no one to tell what to do. Instead, we had to follow everyone else's orders.

As I said, fighting a bargleboar is scary. They are foul tempered. They have very sharp tusks. They have gnashing teeth. They have toxic bad breath. And their favorite hobby is trampling knights into goulash.

But as scary as that was, there was something I was even more afraid of:

Having the other knights *learn* I was scared.

Knights were supposed to be brave. On our brigade, courage was revered and respected, while fear was looked down upon and ridiculed. Tales were told of the heroic exploits of Vincent the Valiant, Hector the Heroic, and Broderick the Bold, while jokes were made about Francis the Fearful, Thomas the Timid, and Lawrence the Lily-Livered.

(Sir Render, a previous member of our brigade, had recently fled from a battle with a bandersplatter, screaming in fright; as punishment, he had been demoted to stable boy and was now routinely mocked by the other knights.)

I did not want to be demoted. Or mocked. So when I was given the order to attack, I attacked.

Belinda and Sir Cuss and Sir Cumference attacked as well, although Belinda did it because she was truly brave, Sir Cumference did it because he was hungry, and Sir Cuss just wanted to stab something. Sir Fass probably would have attacked as well, but he had lost his sword.

However, while the others raced forward with their weapons, I had another trick up my sleeve.

There was one more member of the Knight Brigade: Sir Eberal, who was old and wise and very smart. Instead of fighting vicious beasts, he tried to learn other ways to defeat them. He interviewed village elders and travelers from distant lands and amassed knowledge.

The other knights didn't think much of him. Most of them had joined the brigade so they could destroy things and look valiant while doing it. No one wanted to hear that the best way to defeat a blugslug was to just sprinkle salt on it and watch it dissolve.

Except me.

TWO WAYS TO DEFEAT A BLUGSLUG

I spent a lot of time talking to Sir Eberal about ways to triumph over bloodthirsty beasts that did not involve stabbing. Or gouging. Or any type of messy swordplay. Recently Sir Eberal had heard from a passing horse trader that bargleboars were extremely allergic to paprika.

I know that sounds ridiculous. When I first heard it, *I* thought it sounded ridiculous. But then I remembered that lots of people have very nasty allergic reactions to all sorts of commonplace things. For example, my cousin Mungo swells up like a cow's udder every time he gets near cat dander. And if my aunt Vernetta even touches flaxseed, she gets so many red welts that she looks like a giant raspberry. So it seemed possible that bargleboars might be allergic to paprika, and thus I had tucked a vial of it into the cuff of my armor. (Like I said, I had a trick up my sleeve.)

The problem was, I had to get the paprika to the bargleboar's nose, which was at its front end, where all the other dangerous parts were, like the sharp tusks and the gnashing teeth and the toxic breath. I edged as close as I dared, doing my best to look as though I were brave and gallant and not about to soil myself.

"Stab it!" Sir Vyval yelled from the castle.

"Stab it!" Sir Mount repeated from his horse.

"Yeah!" Sir Cuss exclaimed. "Let's do some stabbing!"

I did not follow their orders. Instead, I took out the vial, uncorked it, and poured some paprika into my hand.

The bargleboar barreled toward me, its hooves thundering on the ground, its deadly tusks gleaming with spittle.

"Tim!" Sir Vyval yelled. "Why aren't you stabbing it?"

"Yeah," Sir Mount seconded. "Why aren't you stabbing it?"

"Have you lost your mind?!" Sir Cuss demanded. "It's stabbing time!"

I ignored them and blew on the paprika. The spice flew from my hand in a great cloud of red . . . just as the bargleboar charged into it.

For a moment, nothing happened. The bargleboar kept coming at me, roaring and drooling, and I figured I had made a terrible mistake and prepared to be trounced into goulash.

But then the bargleboar got a very funny look on its face. It stopped charging. It crinkled its enormous nose.

And then it sneezed. A lot. Huge, earthshaking, volcanic sneezes that blasted massive globs of boar snot from its nostrils.

I tackled Belinda, knocking her out of the way of some of it.

The bargleboar sneezed violently a few more times, and then a green rash appeared on its snout. The beast no longer

looked vicious. Instead, it looked ill. It quickly turned around and raced back into the forest, whimpering sadly.

I got to my feet, feeling proud of myself, and turned to my fellow knights, expecting them to be proud of me as well.

They were not.

Instead, they were quite angry.

None of them had been agile or quick enough to get

out of the way of the bargleboar's sneezes. So they were all now coated with bargleboar snot. Even Sir Vyval hadn't been out of range.

So instead of being congratulated for saving everyone from the bargleboar, it appeared that I was going to end up in trouble for it.

But before that could happen, an even bigger crisis occurred. Which is what this story is *really* about.

CHAPTER TWO

What Had Gone Wrong

Sir Vyval was just beginning a harangue when the town crier appeared.

I'm sure you noticed that IQ Booster arrow. While I might be afraid of bargleboars and other vicious beasts—as well as the other knights finding out about my many fears— I am not afraid of large words. So every once in a while I'm going to use one. But don't worry. You don't have anything to fear yourself, because I will then define the word for you, like this: "harangue" means "a lengthy and aggressive speech." (The next time your parents start complaining to you about something, like forgetting to pick your socks up off the floor because you were engrossed in this book, just say to them "I understand. I don't need to hear a whole harangue about it." They'll be so impressed by your vocabulary that they'll probably forget all about the socks.)

"Your actions were rash and reckless!" Sir Vyval shouted angrily. "And you disobeyed a direct order from me in the midst of battle. . . ."

"But my actions worked . . . ," I pointed out.

"Not as far as I'm concerned!" Sir Vyval roared, pointing to his mucus-coated armor, which he was no longer wearing. (He had already bathed to get the snot off himself but was so angry at me that he hadn't wasted time getting dressed again before starting his harangue. He was now only wearing a towel.) "It's going to take forever to get that clean again. And furthermore, your actions didn't just befoul me and your fellow knights. They also humiliated us! In all my years as head knight I have never been so—"

He probably would have gone on like that for a very long time if the town crier hadn't interrupted him.

The town crier's job was to deliver messages, and since there was very little good news back in olden times, he cried a great deal.

You could tell how bad the news was by how much

the crier was crying. At the time, he was sobbing heavily, which indicated the news wasn't quite as horrible as when Princess Grace had been kidnapped by a monster (uncontrollable wailing) but far worse than when the queen had pricked herself on a rosebush (mild whimpering).

"Excuse me, sir . . . ," he blubbered.

Sir Vyval wheeled on him angrily. "I am delivering a harangue!"

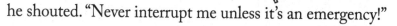

he shouted. "Never interrupt me unless it's an emergency!"

"But it *is* an emergency," the crier bawled. "The queen's golden fleece is missing!"

That news was bad enough to make even Sir Vyval forget about yelling at me. And to forget that he was almost naked as well. "Oh no!" he exclaimed, and then raced for the throne room, wearing only his towel.

Belinda and I followed him. As we passed through the castle, the other knights joined us. They had all been interrupted in the midst of bathing and so were also wearing only towels. Some still had large gobs of boar snot on them.

We arrived in the throne room to find King and Queen Sunderfire, the rulers of Merryland, and their daughter, Princess Grace, waiting for us. King Sunderfire looked worried. Queen Sunderfire was crying. Princess Grace was lurking at the edge of the room.

Sir Vyval asked, "What happened to the golden fleece? Was it stolen?"

"Er . . . no," King Sunderfire admitted uneasily. "Not exactly. It was sort of misplaced."

"Misplaced?" Sir Vyval repeated, confused.

"Yes," the king said. "As you may recall, the king and queen of the Kingdom of Dinkum were here a few nights ago to negotiate a peace treaty with us."

Sir Vyval nodded to indicate that he remembered, as did everyone else in the room. The visit of the king and queen of Dinkum had been a very big deal. Dinkum was a

dangerous kingdom that enjoyed invading other kingdoms. Thankfully, it was located far, far away from us, but negotiating peace had still seemed like a good idea. I'd heard that everything had gone well with the visit . . . until now.

King Sunderfire continued. "As you may also recall, we had a great ball to celebrate the treaty, and my beloved queen dressed in her loveliest gown. However, it was a bit chilly that night, so she donned the golden fleece of Merryland to stay warm. The queen of Dinkum had a golden fleece as well, which looked extremely similar. Well, as the night went on, the two queens sat by the fire and took off their fleeces. And it seems that they got them mixed up. The other queen took *our* fleece back to the Kingdom of Dinkdom . . . I mean, the Dingdom of Kinkum . . . I mean, the Plinkton of Gingham . . ."

"The Kingdom of Dinkum?" Sir Vyval said helpfully.

"Yes!" the king exclaimed. "So I need you to go and get ours back!"

"Oh," said Sir Vyval, looking slightly uneasy. "You are aware that the Kingdom of Dinkum lies across the Sea of Terror, which is filled with dangerous beasts and a great number of other perils?"

"Yes," the king replied. "But our golden fleece is extremely important."

"Can't our queen use the golden fleece that the queen of Dinkum left behind?" Sir Vyval asked. "I'm sure it's very nice."

Queen Sunderfire burst into tears. "It's not the same at all! Mine was very special to me!"

"And to the kingdom," the king added. "You see, our golden fleece wasn't merely dyed gold, like that of the Kingdom of Dinkum. Ours was made of actual gold, which had been spun into delicate fibers. And so, it was worth a great deal of money. In fact, it was worth more than this entire castle."

Everyone gasped in surprise.

"A piece of clothing was worth more than an entire castle?" Belinda whispered to me. "No wonder they call it a 'fleece.'" ⟨ IQ BOOSTER!

(You may not know this, but "fleece" has two definitions. The more common one is "a jacket or garment made of a nice warm fabric." The second is "to obtain a great deal of money from someone by swindling them." So, as you can see, Belinda was making a very clever and hilarious play on words, which is *much* funnier if you know both definitions. Feel free to use it the next time someone tells you how much their golden fleece cost.)

"And also," the king went on, "Queen Sunderfire had left the Mystical Protective Amulet of Merryland in the pocket."

Everyone gasped again, only this time it was more out of worry than surprise.

You see, the Mystical Protective Amulet of Merryland was magic. It had been created by the famous wizard Shaboo the Magnificent long ago and had protected Merryland from grave danger ever since. It exerted a powerful mystical force on humans and was one of the things that had kept the armies of Dinkum away, as well as invaders from other nasty places. Without it, Merryland was in serious trouble.

Yes, we still had the Knight Brigade to defend our kingdom. But as you may have noticed, our brigade was quite small. We had our hands full dealing with a single bargle-boar. Fending off an invading army was well beyond our abilities.

"Yikes," Sir Vyval said. "That's really not good at all."

"I'm so sorry!" Queen Sunderfire sobbed. "But the queen of Dinkum had heard the tales of the amulet and wanted to see it. She asked very nicely, so I had it removed from the royal vault to show it to her—and then I put it in my pocket for safekeeping. It never occurred to me that the queen would take my fleece by mistake!"

"Do you think the king and queen of Dinkum know they have the amulet?" Sir Vyval asked.

"I am guessing that they have not noticed yet," King Sunderfire replied. "And hopefully, they won't until the amulet is safely on its way back to our kingdom. Because even though we have a peace treaty with them, the last thing we need is for a warlike country like the Dinkum of Kingdom to realize that we no longer have our protective amulet. So I am going to need my knights to set sail for the Bingdom of Flinkum right away, then retrieve the amulet before the Dingbum of Klingum even knows you were there."

The knights all exchanged wary glances.

"Er . . . ," Sir Vyval said. "I'm not saying that's a *bad*

plan. But . . . you do know we aren't a navy, right? None of us have ever been to sea. And there are all those monsters and perils to contend with. I mean, it's called the Sea of Terror, not the Sea of Pleasantness. . . ."

"Sir Vyval!" the king bellowed. "Are you afraid of this mission?"

"Afraid?" Sir Vyval scoffed. "I fear nothing, Your Majesty! But I thought that, as the leader of your knights, it was important to point out how dangerous the mission was before I sent them all off on it. . . ."

"Sent them?" the king repeated. "You're not *sending* your knights on this mission, Sir Vyval. You'll be leading them!"

"Me?" Sir Vyval asked. "But shouldn't someone stay behind in case the castle gets attacked by vicious beasts? We're just at the start of bloodmonger season, and you know how nasty they can be. . . ."

"You are the leader of the Knight Brigade!" King Sunderfire roared. "It is your job to supervise my forces on dangerous missions! And this one will require every able-bodied man we have!"

"I can go too!" Princess Grace said suddenly.

Everyone turned to her with their mouths agape.

Princesses were not supposed to volunteer to go on dangerous voyages. They were not supposed to do anything dangerous at all. And if they did end up in trouble, they were supposed to sit tight and wait for a prince to come rescue them. That was the way things had been done for a long, long time.

Of course, that didn't mean it was right.

Princess Grace was not a big fan of the way things had been done.

However, her parents were.

"That is out of the question," the king said.

"But I could help . . . ," Princess Grace began.

"No you could not," the king said sharply. "You are a princess, not a knight. In the first place, only men can be knights . . ."

(As he said this, Belinda looked away and whistled innocently.)

". . . and secondly, no daughter of mine is going on any perilous missions. Your job is to stay here and get into some sort of hazard at home so that a dashing prince can come rescue you and then be given your hand in marriage."

"Ugh," Princess Grace said, making a face.

Queen Sunderfire grew very embarrassed. "Grace! You know we don't like that attitude one bit! It's bad enough that you rejected the hand of that handsome Prince Ruprecht. . . ."

"Prince Ruprecht kidnapped me and locked me in a labyrinth," Grace reminded her.

"Nobody's perfect," the queen replied. "It's high time you met someone. You know, just a few kingdoms away, Princess Aurora met a lovely prince after she pricked her finger on a cursed spinning wheel and went into a coma. After only a century of sleep, the prince came along and kissed her; she woke up, and now they're married."

"Unhappily," Grace added. "Turns out, coma-inducing sewing accidents are not a great thing to base a relationship on."

"I've heard enough of this," King Sunderfire snapped. "I'm not letting you go on this voyage. The Sea of Terror is chock-full of dangerous monsters and horrifying perils, and the chances of anyone surviving a trip across it without being eaten or dying a terrible death are extremely small. This journey will be an endless series of nightmarish encounters that are sure to be the absolute most awful experiences anyone has ever faced. I forbid you to go!"

Then he turned to the Knight Brigade and said, "But you all are doing it. Have fun!"

Which is how I ended up crossing the Sea of Terror.

CHAPTER THREE

How We Got the *Herring*

The king and queen were so desperate to get the golden fleece (and the Mystical Protective Amulet) back that they didn't even give us time to pack.

But then, I didn't have anything to pack anyhow. I was wearing everything that I owned:

My shirt

My pants

My shoes

(The armor and the sword were only on loan.)

Underwear had not been invented yet. Or socks. Or deodorant or toenail clippers or toothbrushes.

That's right. We invented the sword and all sorts of other weapons way before we invented the toothbrush. That ought to tell you everything about humanity's priorities.

The other knights didn't own anything either (except Sir Cumference, who had a strange new item called a fork that he said helped with his dining). They quickly put their armor back on, and then we all began our journey to the Sea of Terror.

Me, Belinda, Sir Vyval, Sir Cuss, Sir Cumference, Sir Fass, Sir Eberal, Sir Vaylance, Sir Mount, Sir Mount's horse, and the stable boy formerly known as Sir Render (who now had to take care of Sir Mount's horse).

My fr-dog, Rover, followed us.

Yes, you read that correctly. Rover was a fr-dog. At one point he had been a dog, but an angry witch

turned him into a frog. So now he was a very large frog that behaved like a dog. He chased cats and buried bones and hated squirrels with the white-hot passion of a thousand suns.

The Sea of Terror was a half day's walk away, which might not sound like much to you, but it was farther than most people in my village had ever traveled in their lives. (You probably wouldn't venture very far from home either if there were bargleboars and blugslugs all over the place.) I had done more traveling than most people, but I still had never been to the harbor. Which meant I had never seen the sea.

Turns out, the sea is really big.

Much bigger than I had ever imagined.

None of the other knights had ever seen the sea before either— except Sir Eberal. So we all stood there for a long time, gawping at it.

"That whole thing is full of water?" I asked, astonished.

"Yes," Sir Eberal replied. "Well, there are also some fish and sea monsters in it. But it's *mostly* water."

"It's shallow, right?" Sir Fass asked hopefully. "So if something happened to our boat, we could just wade back to shore?"

"Er . . . no," Sir Eberal said. "It is much, much, much deeper than that."

"So . . . it would come up to our necks?" Sir Fass asked.

Sir Eberal looked at him like he was a fool. "You have seen Mount Neverest, yes?"

We all nodded. Mount Neverest was the tallest mountain we knew. It was absolutely enormous.

Sir Eberal said, "Imagine a mountain ten times the size of Mount Neverest, then turn it upside down. That's how deep the sea is."

We all gasped at the thought. Except Sir Fass, who asked, "So . . . you're saying it *is* too deep to wade through, then?"

"Yes," Sir Eberal said. "Should something happen to the ship, you will sink into the great, watery depths of the sea, where you will die a miserable death by drowning—unless you are eaten by a sea monster first."

"Yuck," Belinda said. "That sounds awful."

"Sure does," Sir Eberal agreed. "That's why I'm not going."

Belinda and I looked at him, stunned. "You're not coming with us?" I asked. "But you're the smartest member of the Knight Brigade."

"Exactly," Sir Eberal said. "Well, it was nice talking to you. See you when you get back. I mean . . . *if* you get back." He started to slink away.

"The king ordered you to go with us!" Belinda reminded him. "He will be very upset with you if you don't."

"An annoyed king is still far less dangerous than a hungry sea monster," Sir Eberal said.

"But we need your wisdom!" Belinda pleaded.

Sir Eberal paused for a moment. "Just remember that more isn't always better," he said. Then he scurried off and hid behind a tree before Sir Vyval noticed he was gone.

I thought about doing the same thing. This voyage

didn't sound like one bit of fun to me. But then Sir Vyval
noticed the look of concern on my face. "You're not having
second thoughts, are you, Tim?" he asked.

"No," I said, even though I was.

"You're not afraid of going to sea, are you?" Sir Vyval
taunted. All the other knights except Belinda gave me
challenging looks.

"Of course I'm not afraid!" I lied. "In fact, I can't wait
to go! I hope we run into some sea monsters right off the
bat so that we can have some excitement!"

This was called overcompensating. ⟨IQ BOOSTER!⟩ That
means "taking extreme measures to correct or cover up a
weakness or problem." I was so worried about being called
a coward that I pretended to be very brave, rather than
simply admitting the truth.

And now that I had said those things (even though
they weren't really true), the other knights were very quick
to agree, just so everyone knew they were brave too.

"Yes!" Sir Cuss exclaimed. "Let's kill some sea monsters!"

"And eat them!" Sir Cumference added. "I'm sure
they're delicious!"

"Let's get out there and have a great adventure!" Sir Mount declared, making sure he was loud enough for some passing maidens to hear.

"That's the spirit!" Sir Vyval cheered. "Follow me, men!"

We all hurried after him to the edge of the harbor, where there was a small fishing village.

It was so small that there was only one boat, which was docked at the single wharf. The boat was named the *Herring*. I had never seen a boat before,* but even I could tell that this one wasn't exactly top quality, as far as boats were concerned.

---

* If you have read the original *Once Upon a Tim*, you might recall that I *had* seen what I thought was a raft, but which turned out to be something that wasn't a raft at all.

It was old and dilapidated. [IQ BOOSTER!]

"Dilapidated" means "in a state of ruin as a result of age or neglect." Which was certainly the case with the *Herring*. The sails and the hull were covered with patches. The deck was creaky and full of splinters. And as for the figurehead . . . [IQ BOOSTER!] (That's the sculpture carved at the front of the boat.) It had probably been a mermaid at some point, but now it had decayed into something that you'd find lurking under a rock.

The captain of the *Herring* was also old and . . . you're not supposed to use "dilapidated" to describe humans, but in this case, it works.

Sir Vyval was not impressed by the appearance of either one of them. "Hello," he said to the captain. "Are there any other boats in this town?"

"Of course," the captain replied. "There are hundreds. But they're very shy, and so they're all hiding."

"Really?" Sir Vyval asked.

"No, you dimwit," the captain snorted. "Boats don't hide."

All the crewmen laughed at this, which embarrassed Sir Vyval.

"I was just being sarcastic," the captain explained. "The *Herring* is the only boat in these parts."

"Then we'll take it," Sir Vyval said. "Get off right now!"

"You can't take my boat!" the captain exclaimed.

"Oh yes we can!" Sir Vyval announced. "We are the Knight Brigade of Merryland! It is the order of King Sunderfire that we sail at once for the Kinkdom of Blinkum . . . I mean, the Finkdom of Seagum . . ."

"The Kingdom of Dinkum?" the captain asked.

"Right!" Sir Vyval said. "All subjects of Merryland must obey the orders of the king! Also, we have swords and you don't. So get off!"

All of the older knights whipped out their swords. They were very sharp and shiny.

The captain and his crew had no choice but to get off the boat.

"Er . . . ," Belinda said worriedly. "Wouldn't it be a good idea to bring the captain and crew with us? Since they know about boats and the sea?"

"No," Sir Vyval replied. "The captain is a jerk who made fun at my expense. And the crew all laughed at me.

Me, the leader of the knights of Merryland. We have no use for such ungrateful people."

"Are you sure about that?" I asked. "I think we might have a *lot* of use for them. Like sailing the boat. And steering clear of sea monsters."

"How hard can any of that be?" Sir Vyval said with a snort. "Trust me, we will be perfectly fine without them."

Which, of course, turned out to be completely wrong.

CHAPTER FOUR

Why We Got Off to a Bad Start

The problems began right away.

Belinda and I got tangled in the rigging. Sir Vaylance got lost under a sail. Sir Cumference grew seasick the moment we left the dock. Sir Fass somehow got stuck in a barrel. Rover accidentally ate an octopus. Sir Cuss had a seagull poop on his head.

We might never have gotten anywhere if Ferkle hadn't been on board.

We hadn't noticed him right away because he was sleeping in the corner with a bucket over his head.

This was quite common headwear for Ferkle, as he was our village idiot.

However, unlike most village idiots, Ferkle was not actually an idiot. In truth, he was very intelligent. But village idiocy was his family profession. All of his ancestors had been village idiots, and he was expected to follow in their footsteps. (His parents, who were truly idiots, had

been very upset to learn that their son was intelligent, but Ferkle hadn't let that get in the way of his job and had made them very proud.)

Eventually, the sound of Sir Cuss yelling bad words at the seagull woke him.

He sat up and pried the bucket off his head. "Tim?" he asked. "Bull?" (In the Knight Brigade, Belinda used the name Bull so that no one would realize she was a girl.)

"What are *you* doing here?" we asked.

"I'm on my way to the Kingdom of Boobaloo to teach a course in village idiocy," Ferkle explained. "There's a new crop of young idiots who don't know a thing about the profession. A lot of them have never even learned how to properly stick a turnip up their nose."

"There's a proper way to stick a turnip up your nose?" I asked.

"Of course!" Ferkle said, sounding slightly offended. "Village idiocy is a craft. You have to learn the ropes. You start out as a village fool, then work your way up to village moron, then nimrod, numbskull, dumbbell, and fathead . . . and finally, if you're good enough, you can be a village idiot. What are all of *you* doing here?"

Belinda and I explained everything. Ferkle grew more and more concerned as he listened.

"We really need to get that amulet back," he said, once we had finished. "The safety of the entire kingdom depends on it. I suppose I'll have to cancel my visit to the Kingdom of Boobaloo and help out."

I was about to say something like, *That's not necessary. I'm sure we can handle things without you.* But I didn't. For two reasons:

First, I *wasn't* sure we could handle things without Ferkle. Now that Sir Eberal had ditched us, there was no one left on the Knight Brigade with logic or wisdom. The other knights weren't all complete dunces, but their general solution to most problems was to try to stab them. In fact, at that very moment, Sir Vyval was hacking away at the steering wheel in frustration.

Second, I thought I saw a ship following us.

It was quite far away from us, so that it was barely a speck on the horizon, and yet there seemed to be something very sinister  about it. ("Sinister" means "giving the impression that something evil will happen." Like a man-eating bungbear lurking outside your house, licking its lips.) The whole ship was black, from its bow to its stern. Even the sails were black. The sight of it sent a shiver down my spine.

"Do you see that ship?" I asked, pointing.

But as I said it, a cloud passed across the sun, casting that section of the sea into shadow. The ship melted away into the darkness.

"What ship?" asked Belinda.

"I don't see anything," Ferkle agreed.

"It was just there," I said. "Following us."

"Maybe it was a mirage," Ferkle said. "You see those a lot at sea. The sunlight plays tricks on the water."

I wasn't sure what to say. I was quite certain that there had been a ship, but I couldn't see it anymore, no matter how hard I squinted at the horizon. So I figured maybe Ferkle was right. After all, I had never been to sea before; maybe one did see things all the time out here.

I looked toward the front of our boat, just to check if there might be more mirages that way. And sure enough, there was one.

"Ah," I said. "You're right, Ferkle. I'm totally seeing things. It looks like there's a hideous, menacing sea monster ahead of us."

Ferkle and Belinda both looked toward the front of the boat as well.

Then their eyes went wide in fear.

"That's not a mirage," Belinda informed me. "That's an actual sea monster."

"Oh nuts," I said.

CHAPTER FIVE

How We Ended Up in Danger

The sea monster was a good distance away, but still, I could tell that it was not friendly. It was extremely ugly, with long, slimy tentacles, and it had a terrifying look in its eyes—and it was currently eating a small ship that had gotten too close to it.

Unfortunately, the monster was in a narrow passageway between some very steep cliffs, so there did not seem to be a way to get around it.

"Oh," said Ferkle. "That's Scylla. She's a vicious and bloodthirsty sea monster

who devours all ships that come near her."

Belinda looked at Ferkle curiously. "How do you know her name? Or that it's a 'her' at all? Have you met her before?"

"No," Ferkle replied. "It's all in the trip brochure."

"What trip brochure?" I asked.

"The one the captain gives all the passengers when they come aboard," Ferkle said. "See?" He held up a nice, glossy brochure titled "Enjoying Your Voyage on the Sea of Terror."

Belinda said, "I think Sir Vyval must have commandeered the boat before the captain had a chance to give those out."

"Does the brochure offer any handy tips about how to avoid Scylla?" I inquired.

Ferkle quickly consulted the brochure. "Hmmmm. It looks like there are actually *three* narrow passageways ahead, not just one. Scylla is in the first, while Charybdis is in the second. . . ."

"I don't suppose Charybdis is an adorable puppy?" Belinda asked hopefully. "A puppy who just wants to play and lick our faces and not devour anyone?"

"Er . . . no," Ferkle said. "Charybdis is a giant whirlpool that sucks all ships and their passengers down into the inky depths of the sea, making them very dizzy and then crushing them before drowning them in the most horrible death imaginable."

"That is much worse than a puppy," I said. "What's in the third passageway?"

"Fred," Ferkle reported.

"What is Fred?" Belinda asked worriedly. "An acid-spewing volcano that will melt the flesh off our bones?"

"Or a dragon that will swallow us whole and then slowly digest us in its stomach for a thousand years?" I suggested.

"Nope," Ferkle said. "He's just a guy named Fred."

"Is he dangerous?" I asked warily.

"It doesn't appear so," Ferkle replied. "In fact, the brochure says that he's quite friendly and makes an excellent apple pie."

"So our choices are death, death, or pie?" Belinda asked. "This is the easiest decision of all time!"

It seemed that way to me, too. And to Ferkle. And even to Rover, who was just a fr-dog.

Unfortunately, the other knights did not agree.

"I don't like this Fred option at all," Sir Vyval said after we had gotten him to stop hacking at the wheel and explained things to him. "He seems suspicious."

"Suspicious?" I repeated, stunned. "The man seems friendly!"

"And he has pie!" Belinda added.

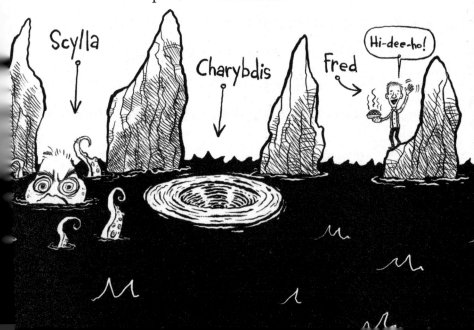

"Exactly," Sir Vyval said. "It sounds like a trap. We'll sail into that passageway, expecting friendliness and a nice slice of pie, and then some horrible monster will emerge from the sea and attack us. I think we're better off facing Scylla."

"But Scylla *is* a horrible monster that will emerge from the sea and attack us!" I pointed out.

"Good," Sir Vyval declared. "That way there are no surprises. Better to face a monster that doesn't try to hide the fact that it's a monster than one that ambushes you while you're having pie."

All the other knights agreed with this, as though Sir Vyval were very wise. Although Sir Cumference seemed quite upset about not getting pie.

By now the other knights finally managed to figure out the basics of sailing, and there was a good wind at our back, so we were heading toward Scylla relatively quickly.

Belinda made a last attempt to talk sense into Sir Vyval. "Sir, Scylla looks extremely dangerous. You can see she is already eating a boat."

"That's a *good* thing," Sir Vyval said. "That means

Scylla is probably full. After I've had a big meal, I get very bloated and tired and just want to lie down and have a nap. I suspect this monster will feel exactly the same way."

"Scylla doesn't look tired at all," I observed.

"And she doesn't look bloated, either," Ferkle said. "In fact, I'd say she still looks ravenous." ◁ IQ BOOSTER !

("Ravenous" means "extremely hungry." It isn't always used to mean hungry for food, though. For example, you could say something like, "After reading the first *Once Upon a Tim* book, I was ravenous for more adventures and devoured the entire series.")

"I don't care how ugly she is," Sir Vyval said. Obviously, unlike you, he had no idea what "ravenous" meant. Then he turned to the other knights and asked, "Who's ready for some stabbing?"

The other knights cheered heartily and waved their swords in the air.

We approached the three passageways. We were close enough to smell the horrible breath of Scylla, and feel the cold winds kicked up by Charybdis, and see Fred as he waved to us and smiled. He was holding a fresh-baked pie in his hands.

"Hi-dee-ho, everyone!" he shouted cheerfully. "I just took this apple pie out of the oven! Would anyone like some?"

"No!" Sir Cuss shouted at him. "We don't want any of your awful pie!"

"Oh," Fred said. "Are you allergic to apples? Because I also made a peach cobbler that's dee-lish!"

"Peach cobbler?" Sir Cumference echoed, drooling. "That sounds amazing! Are we *sure* he's evil?"

"Of course we are!" Sir Vyval roared at him. "We are far too clever to fall for such trickery! Now, let's sail directly toward that bloodthirsty sea monster!"

We were now disturbingly close to Scylla. And getting closer every moment.

I exchanged worried looks with Belinda, Ferkle, and Rover. This all felt like it was going to end very badly. I would have jumped overboard and swum away if I hadn't been wearing heavy armor—and if I had known how to swim.

As the *Herring* approached Scylla, the monster reached for the boat with its slimy tentacles.

Sir Vyval stared it down bravely. "This poor beast doesn't know what it's in for!" he proclaimed. "Men! Start stabbing!"

The other knights raced to the front of our boat, eager to attack. Although Belinda, Ferkle, and I had plenty of opportunity to do some fighting ourselves, since the tentacles were suddenly all around us.

We each plunged our swords into them.

Scylla roared in pain and withdrew all her tentacles.

For a moment, it looked as though Sir Vyval's plan had worked.

And then everything went really, really wrong.

CHAPTER SIX

How Everything Went Really, Really Wrong

Up until that moment, the Knight Brigade had always fought animals on land: bargleboars, munkskunks, horrorhares, and the like. But it turned out there was a big difference between fighting an animal on land and fighting one in the sea:

On land, you can see the entire creature that you're fighting.

It's not like you're ever fighting a land beast and suddenly discover that it's actually ten times bigger than you thought it was. (Although you might discover that it is ten times smellier than you thought, or has ten times more teeth than expected.) But that was what happened now.

The sea trembled. And then the rest of Scylla, which had been hidden beneath the surface of the water, emerged.

The part of Scylla that we had originally thought was the entire monster turned out to be only a tiny fraction of the beast. The creature that we were now facing was a hundred times bigger, a hundred times uglier, a hundred times angrier, and a hundred times hungrier.

Sir Vyval and the rest of the knights suddenly looked far less confident in their decision to attack the monster.

"Oops," Sir Vyval said.

"Don't panic!" exclaimed the stable boy formerly known as Sir Render. "I brought the perfect object to protect us!" He reached into his cloak and removed a white flag, which he waved about wildly. "We give up!" he cried. "Please don't eat us!"

Scylla snatched the flag out of his hand with one tentacle, grabbed all our cannons with the other, then ate the cannons and used the flag as a napkin.

Now shooting the monster was no longer an option.

Not that it would have done any good anyhow. Scylla was so big, and her skin was so thick and scaly, a cannonball would have had the same effect on her that a flea has on a dog.

None of the other knights seemed to have any ideas about what to do. Except Sir Cuss, who suggested, "Let's stab it some more!"

Our situation was very grim.

Scylla loomed over us and roared. Her breath smelled like dead fish and rattled the sails.

But then Ferkle suddenly lit up with excitement, as though he'd thought of a plan. He sprang to the wheel of the *Herring* and spun it as hard as he could. "Help me turn the sails!" he yelled. "Quickly!"

"Hey!" Sir Vyval snapped. "I'm the one who gives the orders around here!"

The rest of us ignored him and leapt to work. Belinda and I ran to the mainsail. The other knights handled the rest of them. The stable boy formerly known as Sir Render curled into a ball and whimpered.

Unfortunately, all the rigging on the mainsail was tangled in a giant ball, so we couldn't use it, but Belinda improvised a very clever solution.

Our actions quickly turned the ship around, so we were now heading away from the hideous sea monster.

Scylla roared. Now the beast's breath filled our sails like the wind and pushed us away. This annoyed Scylla, who roared once more in frustration, which pushed us away yet again. Which annoyed Scylla even more . . .

Scylla wasn't a fool, though. She realized that roaring again would only make the situation worse, so instead she kept her mouth shut and seethed silently.

She still kept coming for us. We had gained a little on her, but she was so big that she quickly closed the gap.

We weren't going to outrace her.

Which was why Ferkle steered right into Charybdis.

Normally, steering a boat into a massive whirlpool of death is a bad idea. (In fact, if you ever train to be a sailor, "Never steer into a massive whirlpool of death" is the second thing you learn, right after "Don't drill holes in the bottom of the boat.") But sometimes, when you are in a very desperate situation—for example, having a massive, ravenous sea monster bearing down on you—you must take some risks.

Everyone else assumed Ferkle knew what he was

doing, as he was very intelligent and seemed to know how to sail a boat, while the rest of us did not. So when Ferkle shouted out orders, we did our best to follow them. (Except Sir Vyval, who was sulking because no one was taking orders from *him*.)

Unfortunately, everything on a boat has a weird name. Even things that already have perfectly good words to describe them. For example, the front of the boat isn't called "the front of the boat." It's called the bow. The back

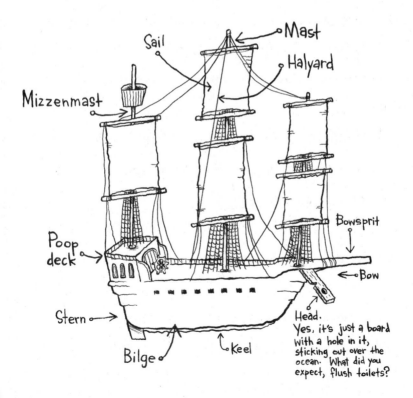

Sail
Mast
Halyard
Mizzenmast
Poop deck
Bowsprit
Bow
Stern
Head.
Yes, it's just a board with a hole in it, sticking out over the ocean. What did you expect, flush toilets?
Bilge
Keel

of the boat is called the stern, the ropes for the sails are called halyards, and the place where you go to the bathroom is called the head. And then, other things have bizarre names like bowsprit, mizzenmast, bilge, and poop deck (which honestly ought to be the name of the place you go to the bathroom).

None of us had learned any of this yet, and there are no helpful IQ Boosters in real life. So we didn't have a clue what Ferkle was talking about.

"Hoist the whangdoodle!" he yelled. (Or something like that.) "Tighten the forgydorfle! Rotate the flutterglump! Don't eat the plurgles!" (This last order was directed to Sir Cumference.)

Even though we didn't fully understand Ferkle, we still tried to obey his orders. The *Herring* continued sailing in the general direction we needed it to.

Charybdis loomed just ahead, while Scylla closed in from behind. The monster's slimy tentacles reached for us . . .

Just as we arrived at the edge of the whirlpool.

Ferkle didn't steer *directly* into Charybdis. Instead,

he kept us at the outer edge. Still, the current caught us and whipped us around quickly, as though we had been dropped into the world's largest toilet.

This sudden burst of speed yanked us out of Scylla's reach. The monster lunged forward to try to nab the boat again and got caught in the whirlpool herself.

Scylla was immediately dragged toward the center of the whirlpool, where the water

was spinning much faster than at the edge. That meant that *Scylla* got spun much faster as well. The giant monster twirled like a top.

Scylla quickly grew dizzy and began to look nauseous.

("Nauseous" really means "ready to vomit." There are lots of things that can make you nauseous. For example: eating raw eels in pickle juice, smelling the armpit of a bungbear, or listening to your parents call each other pet names like Honeybunch or Sexypants. But nothing makes you more nauseous than being spun around really fast.)

Scylla turned green. Well, greener than before. And she made a low, unhealthy moaning noise.

"She's going to blow!" Ferkle warned. "Raise the jim-jammer! Turn the flibbertigibbet! Spangle the whizz-majizz!"

The only thing that might be more frightening than getting eaten by a sea monster is getting barfed on by a sea monster. We all leapt to work and did what we thought Ferkle wanted us to do.

Before Scylla could puke, though, Charybdis yanked the beast down into its inky depths. There was an

enormous blorping noise, and then Scylla was gone.

With Scylla sucked into it, the whirlpool lessened slightly. The *Herring* was able to pull free from its grasp and sail to the safety of calm waters. Only a few moments later, Charybdis started up again, doing its best to suck us back in, but we were now too far away.

To our astonishment, we had survived.

All of us cheered and lifted Ferkle up onto our shoulders. "Hooray for Ferkle!" we yelled. "He saved us!"

"Big deal," Sir Vyval sniffed in a petulant way. ← IQ BOOSTER!

("Petulant" means "childishly sulky or bad tempered." Sir Vyval was obviously upset that his own plan to save us had been a colossal failure, but that didn't excuse his behavior.)

"Let's not celebrate quite yet," Ferkle told the group. "We might have survived, but we still have to get past Charybdis."

We all stopped cheering. Because Ferkle was right. With all our whirling around, we had ended up right back on the same side of Charybdis that we had started on. The whirlpool loomed in our path once again.

Ferkle said, "I recommend that we give the passageway with Fred a shot this time."

"Sounds like a good idea to me!" Sir Cumference said, and everyone else chimed in in agreement.

Except Sir Vyval. "I'm *still* not sure that passage is safe," he said. "I don't trust that Fred character at all. I'll bet that this route turns out to be far more hazardous and deadly than any of you expect."

Despite this warning, we decided to take our chances.

CHAPTER SIX AND A HALF

How We Made It Past Fred

It was actually really easy. And we got pie.

CHAPTER SEVEN

What the Next Big Surprise Was

After we had safely made it past Fred and his delicious pie, we all thought it would be a good idea to look at the map in Ferkle's brochure.

"It would make sense to know what other dangers lie in store for us," Sir Vaylance said.

"And to know the least perilous route to take," Sir Mount put in.

"And to know if there's any more pie ahead," Sir Cumference added hopefully.

"Yes, I think all of that would be very good to be aware of," Ferkle agreed.

Then he unfolded the brochure to display the map inside. It looked like this:

"The sirens?" I asked. "What are the sirens?"

"You've never heard of them?" Belinda asked me, surprised.

"No," I replied. "That's why I asked what they were."

"Oh. Right," Belinda said. "The sirens are horrible creatures that are half-bird and half-woman. They sing the most incredibly beautiful songs, which lure sailors into smashing their boats on the rocks around their island and drowning."

"Yikes," said Sir Cumference.

"Actually, that story isn't quite true," Ferkle corrected. "According to the brochure, the sirens' songs aren't beautiful at all. I mean, why would beautiful songs lure you into smashing your boat on the rocks? Beautiful songs might make you want to dance or sing along, but smash your boat? I don't think so."

"Then why are the sirens so dangerous?" Belinda asked.

"Because their songs are *awful*," Ferkle explained. "They're the most dreadful, appalling, ghastly songs you've ever heard. They're so bad that they make sailors want to smash their boats on the rocks and sink into the sea so that they won't have to listen to them anymore."

"Ah," Sir Fass said. "That makes much more sense."

I thought so too. And yet, I couldn't help but ask, "Could the songs really be that bad?"

"The Kingdom of Dinkum once sent out their navy to destroy the sirens," Ferkle said. "They selected the strongest, bravest, toughest men. None of them made it through the first song. In fact, many couldn't even wait to smash on the rocks. They threw themselves overboard to get eaten by sharks before the sirens even got to the chorus."

"Double yikes," said the stable boy formerly known as Sir Render. "Maybe we should quit and go home."

"We can't do that!" snapped Sir Mount, who was still on his horse for some reason, even though we were at sea. "If we don't get the magical amulet back, *our* kingdom will be in great danger!"

"We can't get the amulet back if we're dead," the stable boy formerly known as Sir Render pointed out. "If we go home, at least we have a chance of survival."

"We are knights!" Sir Cuss reminded him. "We can't turn back! It is our sworn duty to face danger—and stab it!"

The other knights heartily agreed with this.

I did not. After Scylla and Charybdis, I was in no hurry to have another near-death experience. Or an actual death experience. But as I thought about the sirens, an idea came to me. An idea about how to get past them.

Before I could think it through, however, Sir Vaylance pointed to the spot on the map with all the question marks and asked, "What's *this* all about?"

"I don't know," Ferkle replied. "And neither does anyone else, it seems. That's a blank spot on the map."

"No one has ever gone there?" Sir Mount asked.

"Oh, plenty of people have gone there," Ferkle replied. "But no one has come back."

Even the bravest knights among us seemed worried by that.

"I say that we avoid that part altogether, then," Sir Fass suggested.

The other knights heartily agreed with this, too.

"Of course, that still leaves the sirens to deal with," Ferkle said. "I don't think we can escape them so easily. I hear their music carries a long way."

The idea I was working on suddenly came together. "I know how to . . . ," I began.

But then one of the knights sneezed.

Normally this wouldn't have been a very big deal. The knights in our brigade sneezed all the time—and made plenty of noises with other parts of their bodies as well.

However, this sneeze was unusual. It was very high-pitched and dainty.

Everyone grew suspicious at once. "Who just did that?" Sir Vyval demanded.

No one responded.

Everyone carefully studied all the other knights. And then everyone's eyes fell on the one knight who was still wearing their helmet with the visor down over their face.

It suddenly occurred to all of us that there was one more knight aboard than there should have been.

On board we had:

Me

Belinda

Ferkle

Rover

Sir Vyval

Sir Cuss

Sir Fass

Sir Vaylance

Sir Cumference

Sir Mount

Sir Mount's horse

The stable boy formerly known as Sir Render

And one other random knight.

Now before you think I was foolish for not noticing there had been another knight on board all along, let me ask you something: Did *you* notice???

Go back and look at the illustrations of us leaving our village and getting tangled in the ropes on the *Herring* and eating pie. The extra knight is in all those drawings, but I'm guessing you didn't pick up on that either. And you

were simply reading this book in a nice, safe place where you probably didn't have that much else to think about. I had sea monsters and giant whirlpools to contend with.

Anyhow . . .

There was an extra knight on our ship. And I thought I recognized the sound of the sneeze.

"Princess Grace?" I asked. "Is that you?"

"No," the knight said in a voice that sounded very much like Princess Grace trying to sound like someone else. "I'm not Princess Grace. I'm a knight."

"Then what is your name?" Sir Fass asked.

"Uh . . . ," said the mystery person. "Sir . . . um . . . Squirrelblarg."

Belinda said, "Princess Grace, we know it's you."

The knight lifted up the visor on their helmet, revealing that it

was, indeed, Princess Grace inside the armor.

"Princess!" Sir Vyval exclaimed in surprise. "You shouldn't be here! You should be back at the palace, where it's safe!"

"The palace is *boring*," Princess Grace replied. "All I'm supposed to do is wear fancy dresses and have tea and get into trouble so that a prince can come rescue me. The only time I've ever had any fun at all were the times when I was captured by the stinx and by Prince Ruprecht."

"But you were in grave danger on those occasions," Sir Vaylance reminded her.

"And it was *exciting*!" Princess Grace said. "Sure, there were moments when I was scared, but at least I got to *do* something for once."

"I'm turning this boat around and taking you back," Sir Vyval said sternly. "There are perilous perils ahead. This is no place for a young woman."

At this, Belinda averted her eyes and hummed innocently.

Princess Grace folded her arms across her chest and gave Sir Vyval a defiant stare. "I am not going back. In fact, as the princess of Merryland, I demand that you continue this voyage with me aboard."

"I don't answer to you," Sir Vyval informed her. "I answer to the king and queen. And if I let anything bad happen to you, then I'll lose my head."

"I. Am. Not. Going. Back," Princess Grace repeated truculently. ◁ IQ BOOSTER!

("Truculently" means "in an aggressively stubborn manner." Normally, when people behave truculently, it's annoying—although in this case, Princess Grace had good reason.)

"Yes. You. Are," Sir Vyval said bellicosely. ◁ IQ BOOSTER!

("Bellicosely" means "demonstrating aggression and a willingness to fight." When people behave bellicosely, that is also annoying—although in this case, Sir Vyval had good reason. He wasn't kidding about having his head chopped off.)

"No. I'm. Not," Princess Grace replied pugnaciously. ◁ IQ BOOSTER!

("Pugnaciously" means "ready to argue or fight." When you think about it, there are a startling number of words to describe people being in a bad mood.)

Sir Vyval started to say something else in a way that could be defined with a big word, but before he could, Princess Grace cut him off.

"There's no point in going on like this," she told him. "I'll be fine. Now that we're past Scylla and Charybdis, I'll bet we're through the hardest part of this journey. I'm sure nothing could be worse than that."

At which point, everything immediately got worse.

Because we came upon the sirens.

CHAPTER EIGHT

How I Ended Up Volunteering

At first we could barely hear the sirens' singing. It was fainter than a whisper. But even that tiny hint was enough to indicate how incredibly awful the sirens' songs were.

Olden times were not known for our music. The most famous band, the Pied Pipers, were renowned for playing music so bad that it drove rats out of your village.

And yet the sirens were much, much worse.

Everyone cringed so hard that our armor rattled. Sir Mount's horse whinnied in fear. The stable boy formerly known as Sir Render collapsed to the deck in a gibbering heap.

Rover didn't seem too bothered by it, though.

The rest of us were in bad shape. Princess Grace looked as though she had suddenly begun to doubt her decision to come along.

"How are we ever supposed to get past this?" Sir Mount wailed. "I can barely hear it, and I already want to throw myself to the sharks."

"We'll never make it unless we can find some way to avoid hearing this dreadful singing," Belinda said thoughtfully.

"I think I know how to do that," I said, recalling my idea. "Everyone on board will stuff a bunch of candle wax in their ears to block the sound—except for one person, who will be tied to the mast. Then we'll sail our boat past the sirens until the one who can still hear gives the word that it's safe to take the wax out again."

Everyone considered that for a moment.

"I suppose that would work," Sir Fass agreed, "but it would be a nasty ordeal ⟨ IQ BOOSTER! ⟩ for the person who gets tied up."

(An ordeal is a painful or horrific experience and generally a very long one at that. Imagine fighting a bargleboar during a paprika shortage while you have a bad toothache and your pants are three sizes too small. Throw some head lice in there, and you've got yourself an ordeal.)

"That's true," I admitted. "It would be nasty indeed."

The other knights all shared a devious look.

"Then whoever is chosen would have to be extremely brave," Sir Vyval said. "And not afraid to take one for the team."

"Correct," I said.

"So then, I guess *you* wouldn't be interested," Sir Vyval said to me.

This was true. I did not want to suffer through the songs of the sirens. Instead, I had planned to suggest that we all draw lots and randomly select a poor sap who would get tied to the mast.

But as afraid as I was of being the poor sap, once again, I was more afraid of admitting that I was afraid. All the other knights and Princess Grace were looking at me expectantly, and I didn't want them to know that, at heart, I was scared.

So I did something so dim-witted, even a village idiot wouldn't have done it.

I said, "Oh, I would be *very* interested."

Belinda put her hand on my arm. "Wait, Tim. We could select a person randomly. You don't have to volunteer. . . ."

"Unless you're *chicken*," Sir Cuss taunted. And then he flapped his arms like they were wings and said, "Bock bock bock!"

The other knights joined in, flapping their arms and clucking as well.

Rover now looked very confused, as though he suspected that a witch had just turned our brigade of knights into chickens.

I found this all very aggravating. "I am *not* a chicken!" I declared.

Belinda tried to talk sense into me again. "Tim, take a moment. . . ."

But I was too worked up and ignored her. "I'm not afraid of the sirens!" I told the knights. "I can handle being tied to the mast! In fact, I volunteer to do it!"

This would be another example of overcompensating. I was so determined to prove that I wasn't scared that I agreed to do something that terrified me.

It was also something that no one else wanted to do. The moment the words were out of my mouth, the other knights instantly stopped taunting me and grinned, pleased with themselves. As if, perhaps, they had been planning to trick me into volunteering the whole time.

"Sounds like a great plan!" Sir Mount cheered.

"Let's get Tim tied to the mast!" Sir Vaylance said.

"I'll go find some candle wax for the rest of us!" Sir Fass announced.

"Is there any chance the sirens have pie?" Sir Cumference asked.

Everyone ran about, preparing to deal with the sirens.

Except Belinda, who sighed sadly and looked at me like I was a dimwit. "You didn't have to do that," she told me.

"It's no big deal," I replied, even though I secretly felt very foolish. "I can handle it."

Belinda sighed again.

The other knights found some rope and lashed me to the mast. Then they all jammed wax into their ears—and Rover's and Sir Mount's horse's ears as well—to cut out the sound of the sirens, which was getting worse and worse.

"Can anyone hear anything?" asked Princess Grace.

"What?" asked Sir Vyval. "I can't hear you! I have wax in my ears!"

"WHAT WAS THAT, SIR?" Sir Cuss shouted. "I CAN'T HEAR YOU! I HAVE WAX IN MY EARS!"

"WHAT ARE ALL OF YOU TALKING ABOUT?" yelled Sir Fass. "I CAN'T HEAR YOU! THERE'S WAX IN MY EARS!!!!"

It went on like that for a while, until everyone was

hoarse from shouting and decided to just get on with sailing the *Herring*.

We were getting closer to the sirens. And the closer we got, the worse the singing got.

I was already beginning to regret volunteering.

I didn't want to show any weakness, though.

"This won't be so bad," I told myself. "You'll get through it just fine."

I was wrong.

CHAPTER NINE

What the Worst Night of My Life Was Like

I could try to describe how terrible the singing of the sirens was, but I am not sure that words can do it justice. So here is a chart that might help:

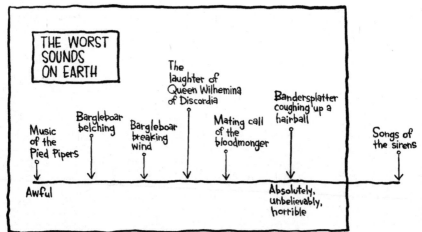

THE WORST SOUNDS ON EARTH

Music of the Pied Pipers

Bargleboar belching

Bargleboar breaking wind

The laughter of Queen Wilhemina of Discordia

Mating call of the bloodmonger

Bandersplatter coughing up a hairball

Songs of the sirens

Awful

Absolutely, unbelievably, horrible

People are often surprised to hear how absolutely horrendous the sirens' singing was, since sirens were half-human and half-bird, and people tend to think of birds as having beautiful singing voices.* But if you think about it, there are plenty of birds with really terrible voices, like ducks. You have probably never heard a duck sing before; this is because they are embarrassed by how awful they sound and worried that other birds will pelt them with seeds or berries to make them stop. Well, imagine a duck trying to sing, and then make it a million times more awful. That's a fraction of how bad the sirens sounded.

And the lyrics were even worse.

The sirens' songs were not about beautiful things like love and honor and sunsets. They were about annoying things like ingrown toenails and having sand in your shorts and waiting in line at the department of motor vehicles. I do not even know what the department of motor vehicles is, but the sirens' song made it sound like it was some sort of ghastly torture from the future. Although it couldn't

---

* Often, over the course of history, important details get altered. I'm guessing that much of what you've heard about my time was wrong. Sometimes this is due to people just getting the facts mixed up through the years, although sometimes it is also due to public relations. For example, I am guessing you might have heard of a princess from my time named Snow White who a magic mirror claimed was "the fairest of them all." That's a load of hooey. Snow White wasn't fair in the slightest; in fact, she was famed throughout the land for cheating at cards.

possibly be as ghastly as listening to the sirens.

As if the music and lyrics weren't bad enough, there was also a complete lack of harmony. All the sirens were singing entirely different terrible songs at the same time. That meant that I wasn't merely listening to a horrendous power ballad about filthy armpit hair, but also a gloomy tune about maggots, a downbeat ditty about swamp gas, and a moody solo called "Does This Look Infected to You?" The resulting cacophony of caterwauling ⟨ IQ BOOSTER! was nauseating.

(You probably remember learning "cacophony" from one of my previous adventures: "a harsh, discordant mixture of sounds." "Caterwauling" is "making a shrill or wailing noise." And, for the record, repeating a similar sound in a phrase, such as the hard *c* in "a cacophony of caterwauling" is called "consonance." "Consonance" can also be used to refer to musical harmony and is thus the opposite of "dissonance," which is the perfect description of the sirens' singing.)

After only a short time being tied to the mast and forced to listen to all this, I wanted to tear my ears off. I would have been happy to go deaf for the rest of my life rather than hear any more of the sirens' screeching voices and nauseating lyrics. The songs made my eyes water and my skin crawl. I was in total and utter agony.

Meanwhile, everyone with their ears plugged seemed to be having a lovely time.

The wax worked perfectly. No one else could hear a thing. And except for the music, it was a pleasant night on the Sea of Terror: the weather was warm with a slight breeze, the sky was clear and full of stars, the water was calm, and no sea monsters were trying to eat us. The gentle rocking of the *Herring* on the waves lulled most everyone to sleep, while Sir Fass and Sir Cuss, who were stationed at the helm, looked relaxed and happy—and Sir Cuss rarely looked happy about *anything*.

Throughout the night, I regretted how easily I had been tricked into suffering through the sirens' songs. The music drove me to despair. I writhed and thrashed against my bonds, hoping to break free and knock myself uncon- scious before I had to listen to one more verse of "The Potato Blight Blues." However, the ropes held me tight. I couldn't escape.

At some point we came dangerously close to the island, and I caught a glimpse of the sirens on the shore. They were almost as monstrous as their music. The half of them that was a bird wasn't even a beautiful bird, like a peahen. Nor was it a majestic bird, like an eagle. Instead, the half-bird parts were all really weird birds, like ostriches and penguins and pelicans.

Now that we were close, they became even more determined to get us to smash onto the rocks of their island. So their songs grew even worse, which I hadn't thought was possible. It was torturous.

That single night felt like a thousand years.

Eventually, thankfully, we made it past the island, and the sound of the sirens' songs began to fade. As the sky started to lighten, signaling dawn was coming, their voices grew fainter and fainter. By the time the sun peeked over the horizon, they were only a distant murmur.

I was thinking it wouldn't be long until I could tell everyone we were finally safe . . .

And then I saw the black ship again.

It was way off in the distance, so far away it was very small. But once again, I had a feeling of menace when I saw it.

And then the sun came up just a bit more, and the black ship vanished in the gleam of light on the water.

I was still concerned, though. And I would have told everyone about it right away if I hadn't noticed something else.

I could no longer hear the sirens' horrid songs.

Instead, I heard something that was actually *worse*.

CHAPTER TEN

How My Plan Failed

There was roaring in the distance.

Not the roaring of hungry lions, which would have been bad enough.

And not the roaring of bloodthirsty beasts that were half-lion and half–something else, like sphinxes or stinxes or manticores, which would also have been bad.

This was the roaring of water. A LOT of water, pouring over the edge of a cliff and then smashing into rocks far, far below.

We had unwittingly sailed into the unknown area of the map. And now I had a very good idea why no one had ever come back from there: a massive, deadly waterfall lay ahead.

If we went over it, the *Herring* would be destroyed, and we would all be fish food. Unfortunately, neither Sir Fass nor Sir Cuss could hear the sound of approaching doom because they still had wax jammed in their ears.

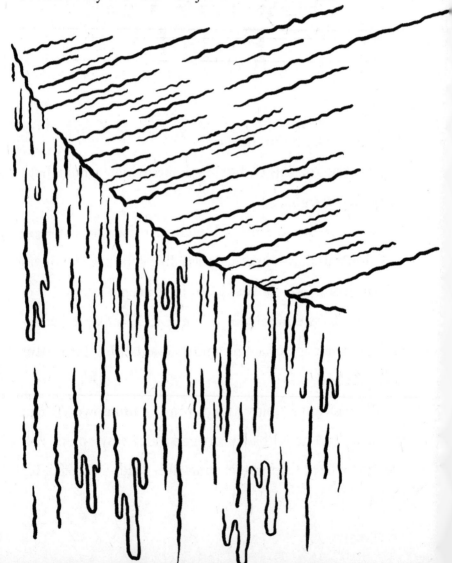

"Hey!" I yelled at them. "We're past the sirens! But now we are heading for a massive, deadly waterfall! We need to turn around!"

But of course no one heard that, either. Because they all still had wax jammed in their ears.

"HEY!" I shouted at the top of my lungs. "IT'S SAFE TO TAKE THE WAX OUT NOW!!! BUT IT'S NOT SAFE TO KEEP SAILING IN THIS DIRECTION!!! SO WE REALLY, REALLY, REALLY NEED TO TURN AROUND!!!"

No one heard that, either.

Sir Fass and Sir Cuss did notice me shouting, though. Sir Cuss approached me with a knowing grin on his face.

"I know what's going on here," he said, sounding very pleased with himself. "You're trying to talk us into taking the wax out of our ears. The sirens' songs have driven you mad, and now you want me to fall prey to them as well so that I will steer into the rocks and put you out of your misery. But I'm too clever to fall for that."

"NO NO NO!" I yelled. "YOU AREN'T BEING CLEVER AT ALL! YOU'RE BEING THE OPPOSITE

OF CLEVER! THIS IS NOT A TRICK!"

Sir Cuss laughed. "I wish you could see how silly you look, screaming your head off and trying to fool me. But I can't hear a word you're saying! Ha-ha-ha!"

I gaped at him, stunned that my shrewd plan to get past the sirens was backfiring.

So I tried shouting at everyone else, hoping to rouse someone who was smarter than Sir Cuss or Sir Fass. "HEY, EVERYBODY!" I yelled. "WAKE UP! WE ARE PAST THE SIRENS BUT ARE NOW HEADING FOR A VERY DANGEROUS WATERFALL!"

No one woke up. They remained stubbornly asleep. Even Rover.

Sir Cuss continued laughing at me. "Look at him!" he said to Sir Fass. "Isn't he funny? He's so angry and terrified!"

"WHAT?" Sir Fass yelled back. "I CAN'T HEAR YOU! I HAVE WAX IN MY EARS!"

"WHAT?" Sir Cuss yelled back. "I CAN'T HEAR YOU! I HAVE WAX IN MY EARS!"

"FORGET ABOUT YOUR EARS!" I yelled. "USE YOUR EYES! LOOK TOWARD THE HORIZON!!!

SEE WHERE THE EARTH LOOKS LIKE IT
ENDS? THAT'S BECAUSE THE EARTH *DOES*
END THERE!"

"Ooh!" Sir Cuss said to Sir Fass, staring at my mouth.
"I think I can tell what Tim's saying by reading his lips!"

"GREAT!" I yelled. "THEN TURN THE BOAT
AROUND BEFORE WE ALL DIE!"

"He said, 'Bait!'" Sir Cuss reported. "'Then burn a
gloating clown before skee ball flies!'" He paused to con-
sider that, then frowned at me. "I think those sirens have
made him go crazy. He's not making any sense at all."

At that moment, I *did* go crazy. Because I was so
frustrated and angry and scared. I couldn't believe that
I might have gone through the whole torturous night
listening to the sirens only to die senselessly the next
morning. So I started screaming random words at the
top of my lungs, hoping that *something* I said would get
someone to pay attention to me. "NINCOMPOOP!"
I hollered. "FLUGELHORN! GERRYMANDER!
DONNYBROOK! SNAPDRAGON! COPROLITES!
SPATULA!"

Finally, all my shouting got through to someone: Rover. I suppose because dogs (and fr-dogs) have slightly better hearing than humans.

My fr-dog raised his head drowsily, shook the sleep from his enormous eyes, stretched . . . and then started licking himself.

"ROVER!" I yelled. "THANK GOODNESS YOU'RE UP! WAKE FERKLE. OR BULL. OR SOMEONE WHO KNOWS WHAT THEY'RE DOING!"

Rover did not wake anyone. Instead, he stared at me vacantly with his huge tongue lolling out of his mouth.

I found myself wondering what he could possibly be thinking.

But I figured I would never know.

What Rover Was Thinking

Dum de dum de dum. Doo be doo be doo. Dum de dum de dum. Doo be doo be doo. Dum de dum de dum. Doo be doo be doo. Dum de dum de dum. Doo be doo be doo. Dum de dum de dum. Doo be doo be doo. Dum de dum de dum. Doo be doo be doo. Dum de dum de dum. Doo be doo be doo. Dum de dum de dum. Doo be doo be doo. Dum de dum de dum. Doo be doo be doo. Dum de dum de dum. Doo be doo be doo. Dum de dum de dum. Doo be doo be doo. Dum de dum de dum. Doo be doo be doo. Dum de dum de dum. Doo be doo be doo. Dum de dum de dum. Doo be doo be doo. Dum de dum de dum. Doo be doo be doo. Dum de dum de dum. Doo be doo be doo. Dum de dum de dum . . .

Hey. What's that loud roaring noise?

I hope it's not a big cat. Cats are the worst . . .

Except for squirrels. I hate squirrels!!!

Oh! The roaring isn't coming from a big cat at all. It's only coming from a giant, deadly waterfall at the edge of the earth. That's not so bad.

Dum de dum de dum. Doo be doo be doo. Dum de dum de dum. Doo be doo be doo. Dum de dum de dum. Doo be doo be doo . . .

Wait.

A giant deadly waterfall at the edge of the earth *is* bad! WAKE UP EVERYBODY!!! WAKE UP NOW!!! IF YOU DON'T WAKE UP, WE'RE GOING TO DIE!!!!

CHAPTER ELEVEN

What Went Wrong Next

Thankfully, Rover didn't merely bark. He also ran about the deck, stumbling over the sleeping knights, which roused them from their slumber. Most of them were annoyed by this.

"I was having a wonderful dream, and you ruined it, you freak of nature," Sir Vyval snapped. "Do that again and I'll stab you." Then he lay back down to go to sleep again.

However, Princess Grace sensed that something was upsetting my fr-dog.

"What is it, Rover?" she asked, concerned. "What's wrong?"

"BARK BARK BARK BARK BARK!" said Rover. Then he ran to the bow of the *Herring*.

Princess Grace followed him there and saw the massive dangerous waterfall at the edge of the world ahead of us. "Oh my," she said. Then she scampered about the boat, trying to get everyone's attention.

The knights were much more willing to listen to a worried princess than an agitated fr-dog. There was a lot of confusion at first, as everyone was sleepy, and no one could understand one another because they all still had wax in their ears. But soon the other knights realized what the trouble was, pulled the wax out, cut me loose, and then went to work, desperately trying to avoid the deadly waterfall ahead.

Ferkle took the wheel and shouted orders, and we raced about, tightening lines and unfurling sails. By this point, the current had caught us. We all worked hard to turn the *Herring* around, but even after that, we were still getting pulled toward the edge.

"Everyone grab an oar and start rowing!" Ferkle ordered.

No one questioned this. Not even Sir Vyval, who had finally realized Ferkle knew what he was doing. We each grabbed oars and rowed as hard as we could.

The *Herring* came dangerously close to the edge of the world.

If there had been one less person aboard, we might have gone over. But with the entire brigade

working together, we managed to pull away from the edge.
Then we kept at it, our muscles straining, rowing as hard
as we could, until we left the waterfall behind and made it
back to calmer waters.

It was quite an ordeal. By the time we were finally safe
again, we were exhausted.

Everyone collapsed on the deck, worn out, but happy
to be alive.

"Good boy, Rover," Belinda said, scratching my fr-dog
behind the ears. "You saved us!"

Rover gave her a friendly lick on her
face. And then he licked everyone else's
face too, without even moving from
where he was sitting. Because

his tongue was long enough for
him to do that.

"That fr-dog is a hero!" Sir
Cumference announced.

"Unlike Tim," Sir Cuss said,

then gave me an angry glare. "Why didn't you tell us about the waterfall?"

"I *tried*!" I exclaimed. "But you wouldn't listen to me!"

"How could I listen to you?" Sir Cuss asked nastily. "I had wax in my ears!"

We might have kept on arguing all day if Sir Vaylance hadn't called out from the crow's nest. "Land ho!" he yelled. "The Kingdom of Dinkum is ahead!"

We all looked to the horizon. Sure enough, we could see the green hills of Dinkum in the distance.

I had never been so happy to see anything in my life.

Even though we now had a good wind behind us and we were tired, we still picked up our oars and rowed again anyhow, wanting to get off the Sea of Terror as fast as we could.

After a little while, we were close enough to see villages on the hills, and then we could see individual buildings in the villages, and then we could even see individual people moving about the buildings.

Dinkum was a much larger and richer kingdom than Merryland. The castle was more majestic. The villages had more buildings. And when we got to their harbor, we saw they had many more ships than we did, and they were much bigger than the *Herring*, with awe-inspiring names like the *Intrepid* and the *Dauntless* and the *Amazingness*. The ships were crewed by professional sailors in well-tailored uniforms.

Many of the sailors snickered as we passed, as though they found our ragtag band of knights and our tiny boat amusing.

Eventually we made it to the wharf in the harbor.

To our surprise, the king and queen of Dinkum were waiting for us there, along with a large royal retinue. ⟨ IQ BOOSTER

(A "retinue" is a group of advisers, assistants, and other workers who accompany an important person. In this case, the Royal Retinue of Dinkum had knights, archers, counselors, handmaidens, minstrels, trumpeters, stable boys, pigeon wranglers, jesters, wizards, and dozens of other people as well. It was all very impressive—which is really the whole point of a retinue. I mean, if you're not trying to impress people, you can probably leave the whole gang back at the castle.)

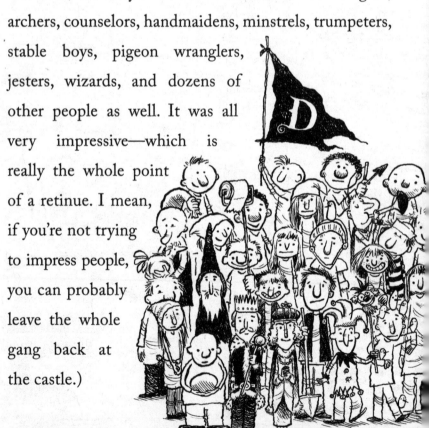

A very joyful-looking man stepped forward. "Hello, good people of Merryland!" he exclaimed. "I am the town laugher, and I—"

"Sorry," interrupted Sir Vyval. "Did you say town *laugher*?"

"Yes!" the jubilant man said. "We used to have a town crier, but the king found him very depressing. So he was sent away, and I replaced him. It is my job to deliver the news with much more happiness and glee, and to pep it up with the occasional chuckle, like so: ha-ha-ha!"

"That *does* sound better than the crying," I whispered to Belinda.

"Yes," she agreed. "Kind of makes you wonder why we have a town crier at all."

The other members of our Knight Brigade seemed equally impressed.

"Anyhoo," the town laugher went on cheerfully, "we spotted your ship from our castle and figured you were probably here about the whole mix-up with the golden fleeces. Ho-ho-ho! Is that right, Princess Grace?"

All eyes turned to the princess. She suddenly looked

unusually self-conscious, perhaps because she was wearing an ill-fitting suit of armor instead of a royal gown, or maybe because her own retinue was a small group of knights, a fr-dog, and the village idiot. (Now that we were in front of other people, Ferkle had gone back to work and had put a live mackerel on his head.)

"Er, yes," Princess Grace replied. "That's correct. We brought your golden fleece back and were hoping to swap it for my mother's."

"Ha-ha!" the town laugher chortled knowingly. "Thought so! We have your mother's fleece on hand! Hee-hee! Royal fleece bearer, please step forward!"

"They have someone whose whole job it is to bear the fleece?" Belinda whispered to me, impressed. "Wow. This is one wealthy country!"

Sure enough, an equally happy woman stepped forward holding the royal golden fleece of Merryland.

It was easy to see how the two fleeces had gotten confused. They looked very similar.

Princess Grace smiled with relief when she saw her mother's golden fleece. "Oh! That's it! And we have yours right here!" She held up the royal fleece of Dinkum, which had been left behind in Merryland.

"Ha-ha!" the town laugher giggled approvingly. "Let the exchange of fleeces begin!"

With much ceremony, he and the royal fleece bearer strode up the gangplank onto the deck of the *Herring*. The royal trumpeters played a triumphant fanfare. The pigeon wranglers released a flock of ceremonial pigeons. One of the pigeons pooped on Sir Cuss, who shouted some very nasty things after it. And then the fleeces were swapped.

Princess Grace eagerly accepted the fleece of Merryland, then quickly checked the pockets.

A worried frown creased her face. Her eyes went wide with fear.

Sir Vyval rushed to her side. "What's wrong, Princess?" he asked.

"The royal amulet is gone!" the princess cried.

CHAPTER TWELVE

What Happened to the Amulet

All the knights gasped in horror at once.

"Is there a problem?" the town laugher asked, although he did so in the most pleasant way possible.

"I'm afraid so," Princess Grace replied. "There was something in the pocket of this fleece: an amulet. It was a large gemstone on a long golden chain. . . ."

"Ah yes," the town laugher replied. "I know exactly what you're talking about. Ha-ha! The queen of Dinkum found it. And then decided not to give it back."

All the knights gasped in horror again.

Princess Grace gave the town laugher a very hard stare. "Why did your queen decide that?" she demanded.

"Well, the amulet was very pretty," the town laugher said. "And it seemed to be very valuable as well. Plus, the

queen had heard rumors that it might have magical qualities that would protect the entirety of any kingdom that
owns it. So we are keeping it. Hee-hee!"

Sir Vyval bristled angrily. "You can't just keep the
Mystical Protective Amulet of Merryland!"

"Of course we can! Ho-ho!" snickered the town laugher.
"Our kingdom's motto is 'Finders Keepers (Losers Weepers)'!
It's right on our royal crest!"

He pointed to the fancy
crest on his uniform. Sure
enough, the motto was
right there.

"Oh," said the stable
boy formerly known as Sir
Render. "I guess we can't argue
with that. It's on a crest."

"That doesn't make it right!" Belinda exploded. "What
if we wrote something on our crest like, 'Welcome to
Merryland—give us all your money'?"

"That's not a bad idea!" Sir Mount said excitedly. "We
should do that!"

Sir Vyval was still glaring at the town laugher. "I don't

care what your crest says. I'm taking our amulet back!" He
drew his sword and pointed it at the man's chest.

An instant later, every one of the knights of Dinkum drew
their swords. Every one of the archers of Dinkum aimed their
arrows. Every one of the sailors aboard the ships of Dinkum
aimed their cannons. And every one of the catapult manag-
ers of Dinkum (who I hadn't noticed until that point, as

they were rather far away) aimed their catapults. At us.

"I wouldn't start stabbing anyone if I were you. Ha-ha!" the town laugher threatened happily. "Because we will kill you instantly. Ho-ho-ho!"

Sir Vyval considered the swords and arrows and cannons and catapults aimed our way. "That is a very good point," he said weakly.

"It would be a wise idea for you to head back to Merryland now. Hee-hee!" the town laugher said.

"Yes," Sir Vyval agreed. "It seems that way. Well, thanks for having us!" He waved goodbye.

"It's been our pleasure," the town laugher said. And then he laughed in a mean, menacing way, like bad guys do when they have just done something really awful to you. "Mwah-ha-ha-ha!"

The king and queen of Dinkum and the entire retinue laughed that way as well.

"MWAH-HA-HA-HA!" they all said at once.

The royal retinue of Dinkum then started back for the castle. Although all the knights and archers and sailors remained behind, pointing their weapons at us.

"Prepare to set sail!" Sir Vyval ordered.

"No!" Princess Grace told him. She was seething mad. "We cannot leave without the mystical amulet!"

Sir Vyval leaned in close to her and whispered, "We aren't."

"It certainly *looks* like we are," Princess Grace snapped. "You just gave orders to leave the Dinkum of Kingbum! I mean, the Brinkum of Dingdong! I mean the . . . Oh! Why does this horrid place need such a ridiculous tongue twister of a name?"

"It may *look* like we are leaving," Sir Vyval whispered to her. "But we are not. We are only making the Dinkums *think* we are leaving. And then we are going to steal our amulet back!"

"Ooh," Princess Grace said, sounding excited.

"Ooh," the other knights echoed, sounding excited as well.

"Uh-oh," I said, very quietly, not nearly as excited as the rest of them.

I was worried that this would be very dangerous.

And I was right.

CHAPTER THIRTEEN

What Our New Plan Was

Ferkle was the first one to voice concerns about the plan. After all, he was the smartest of us, even if he had put a bucket of live eels down his pants.

"How are we supposed to steal the amulet?" he asked. "Did you see the size of the Dinkum army?"

"We don't have to worry about the Dinkum army," Sir Vyval said dismissively. "They don't protect the valuable items in this kingdom. What we *really* need to worry about is the hydra."

"Hydra?" I said, gulping audibly. "You mean, the giant monster that is so deadly and bloodthirsty that all other monsters are terrified of it?"

"Yes," Sir Vyval replied. "They have one here that is

trained to protect all the treasure of Dinkum. See? It's right here on the map."

He held up the brochure that Ferkle had found. It turned out there was an additional flap of the map that the rest of us hadn't noticed before. Sir Vyval now opened it.

"Yikes," Belinda said. "That looks very dangerous."

"I don't think it's anything to worry about," Sir Vyval said confidently. "A lot of this is probably hype to scare thieves away. You can't believe everything you read."

"I never do," Sir Fass said supportively. "In fact, I can't even read in the first place."

"That's the spirit!" Sir Vyval said.

"This hydra doesn't look so bad," Sir Cuss observed. "I'll bet a good old-fashioned stabbing should take care of it."

"Er . . . that didn't work so well against Scylla," Princess Grace reminded him.

Sir Mount waved this off dismissively. "Need I remind you, Princess, that you are a princess and not a knight. So you don't know much about stabbing things. Usually, it works very well. I say we kill this hydra and get our amulet back!"

The other knights agreed. Ferkle, Belinda, Princess Grace, the stable boy formerly known as Sir Render, and I thought this was a mistake, but we were outnumbered, not that the knights would have let us vote anyhow. At Sir Vyval's orders, we sailed out of the Dinkum harbor until no one on shore could see us anymore, and then, instead of heading back toward Merryland, we secretly went in the other direction.

We took the *Herring* around a point of land to a much
smaller harbor shielded from sight by large rocky outcrop-
pings. We anchored there, paddled to shore in our rowboats, then snuck across the countryside until we came
within sight of the hydra.

It was very scary-looking.

As you can see, it was a
large animal with sharp
teeth and long claws,
and even from a
distance, it appeared
to have a very nasty
disposition. ⟨ IQ BOOSTER!

(A "disposition" is
someone's inherent
qualities of mind and
character. For example, a teacher with
a nasty disposition would probably not look kindly upon
you giggling in class while reading a hilarious book, while
a teacher with a sunny disposition would be very pleased
to see that you were reading and might even find the jokes

funny as well. Obviously, the sunny disposition is much more preferable.)

The hydra was protecting a small tower. In the top window, we could see the mystical amulet of Merryland glinting in the sun.

Everyone else saw it too. The other knights grew very upset.

"How dare the Dingdum of Kinklum steal our amulet!" Sir Mount shouted.

"When we steal it back, we should take their other treasure too!" Sir Vaylance declared.

The elder knights chimed in in agreement at the top of their lungs.

"That's a great idea!" Sir Cuss exclaimed.

"It'll serve them right for being such a bunch of lousy thieves!" shouted Sir Mount.

"They'll rue the day they ever decided to mess with the Kingdom of Merryland!" bellowed Sir Mount's horse.*

All this shouting got the hydra's attention. It bared its

---

* I had discovered on a previous adventure that horses can actually talk, although they rarely feel like doing it. But Sir Mount's horse had apparently gotten caught up in the excitement at this point.

teeth and growled angrily. Long strands of drool dripped from its mouth to the ground.

Attacking the beast seemed like a *very* bad idea to me. But I was worried that if I said anything, the elder knights would mock me for being a chicken. Just like they had on the boat. As it was, they were full of anger and ready to cause trouble.

"All right!" said Sir Vyval. "On the count of three, we attack! One . . . two . . ."

"Wait!" Ferkle yelled. "I don't think this is a very good idea."

I sighed with relief, thankful that someone else had been brave enough to say this.

As I had expected, the elder knights gave Ferkle disdainful looks.

"Are you saying that you're too big a chicken to defend the honor of Merryland?" Sir Vyval asked.

"No," Ferkle replied. "I'm saying that this is a bad plan. Attacking that hydra is suicidal."

"You are a coward!" Sir Vyval roared angrily, and all the elder knights agreed.

"Whatever," Ferkle said, not really caring. "I'm sitting this one out." And he sat down on a rock.

"Me too," Belinda said.

"You're *both* cowards!" Sir Vyval accused, and the rest of the elder knights agreed once more.

"Ruff," said Rover, and sat down beside Belinda.

"And you're also a coward!" Sir Vyval told my fr-dog.

"You're the most cowardly beast I've ever seen! All of you have not a single ounce of courage!"

"But they have plenty of intelligence," Princess Grace said. "And I'm staying with them."

"Then you're also a cow . . . ," Sir Vyval began, then realized he was talking to the princess and grew embarrassed. "Er . . . not a cow. Or a coward. Because a princess isn't supposed to fight. That's our job. So sitting and watching us doesn't reflect poorly on you one bit. In fact, it makes you look very regal and important. Unlike these three cowards." He pointed to Ferkle and Belinda and Rover. And then, obviously feeling as though he'd made a fool of himself, he tried to change the subject by wheeling on me. "You've been awfully quiet! What's wrong? Are you too big of a chicken to stand up for your kingdom as well?"

The other knights began to act like chickens again.

The hydra licked its lips hungrily, perhaps thinking that the knights were indeed very large chickens.

I was now positive that attacking the hydra was an extremely bad idea. I desperately wanted to refuse to attack in the same way that my friends had.

But I wasn't as brave as they were. I was still too afraid that the other knights would look down on me for my cowardice.

So instead of admitting that I was scared—or pointing out that attacking the hydra was a very flawed plan—I overcompensated once again.

"Of course I'm not chicken!" I exclaimed. "I've just been quiet because I've been so angry at Dinkum that I couldn't speak! We need to get that amulet back and teach this kingdom a lesson! So let's get that hydra!"

Ferkle, Belinda, and Princess Grace looked at me like *I* was the village idiot.

But the other knights seemed proud. They roared with approval and patted me on the back.

"That's what I like to hear!" Sir Vyval shouted. "At least one of my young charges has some guts! Attack!"

At his words, the other knights whooped excitedly and charged toward the hydra, unsheathing their swords and waving them in the air. I got caught up among them and ran along, yelling and waving my sword the same way that they were.

Although the whole time I was regretting my decision.

Sir Mount, being the only one of us with a horse, got to the hydra first.

The hydra gnashed its teeth, scraped the ground with its claws, then lunged at Sir Mount.

Sir Mount swung his sword . . .

And cut the hydra's head off.

He didn't even
swing that hard.
And yet his
blade still sliced
cleanly through
the hydra's neck.
The head came off
with a slight pop,
like a cork being fired from
a champagne bottle, and then
tumbled to the ground, looking
rather confused about what had
happened.

Sir Mount looked a bit surprised himself. "Gosh," he
said. "That was easy."

The other knights surrounded him, cheering and
chanting his name.

I cheered as well, thinking that everything had worked
out quite well. The elder knights didn't know that I had
been scared—and I was still alive. It appeared that I had
made the correct choice.

But then, while the knights were celebrating around me, I noticed something very strange.

As far as I knew, when you cut something's head off, it was supposed to fall over and die.

The hydra was not doing this.

It was still standing upright. And in the spot where its head had been, its neck looked quite odd.

Something seemed to be growing very quickly there.

Two things, actually.

Before my eyes, where there had been only one head before, two more were taking its place.

And each one of them looked like it had an even worse disposition than the first.

Sir Mount hadn't killed the hydra at all.

Instead, he had made it even more dangerous.

And now it attacked us.

CHAPTER FOURTEEN

How We Made Things Even Worse

The hydra roared with both heads. Each head had a very loud roar, and together, they were earsplitting.

The knights stopped celebrating around me and gasped with surprise.

The hydra charged at us.

Sir Cuss quickly lopped off one of its heads. *Pop!*

Sir Vyval lopped off the other. *Pop!*

And then, almost as quickly, four heads grew back in their places.

These heads were even angrier than the two heads they had just replaced.

The hydra roared with all four of them, which was deafening.

Then it charged again.

Sir Fass, Sir Cumference, Sir Vaylance, and the stable boy formerly known as Sir Render cut off the four heads. *Pop! Pop! Pop! Pop!*

You can probably see where this is going.

Within no time, the hydra had *eight* heads, all of which were absolutely furious. Each head was on a very long neck, so the single hydra could completely surround us.

I ran for my life.

Perhaps you think this was a very cowardly thing to do.

I tell you what: the next time *you* find yourself surrounded by a vicious, angry, eight-headed beast that

refuses to die when you cut its head off, feel free to stand your ground. But if you *do* run, I hope there's not someone reading about it, sitting in a nice, comfy chair in a nice, cozy place, judging you for saving your own life.

For the record, I wasn't the only one who ran. All the other knights did too. Even the dimmest of them had realized that we were in serious trouble. And yet none of them grasped that cutting off the hydra's heads was a losing strategy. The hydra pursued us as we fled, and the knights kept lopping off heads.

Pop! Pop! Pop! Pop! Pop! Pop! Pop! Pop!

Now, the hydra had *sixteen* heads, each of which was infuriated.

This might be a good time to talk about exponential growth. ⟨ IQ BOOSTER !

This isn't really a definition so much as a mathematical explanation. As you may have noticed, we kept doubling the number of heads the hydra had. Repeatedly doubling a number like this is an example of exponential growth. (Obviously, so would tripling or quadrupling the number of heads.) Here is a story to give you an idea of how astoundingly fast exponential growth is:

Long before I was born, a young man gave his king a chessboard as a gift. The king was very pleased and asked if the young man would like anything in return. "Sure," said the young man. "I would be happy if you gave me a single grain of rice for the first square on the board, then two for the second, and kept doubling it until you got to the final square."

The king thought this sounded like a great deal. It barely seemed like he would have to give up any rice at all! So he agreed.

Which turned out to be a very bad idea. Because the king did not understand exponential growth. There are sixty-four squares on a chessboard. By the time that grain of rice had been doubled sixty-three times, the total number of grains was 18,446,744,073,709,551,615. That was basically an entire mountain range of rice. The king and his kingdom went bankrupt paying the young man, who ended up with more food than he had any idea what to do with and died shortly thereafter from a rice overdose.

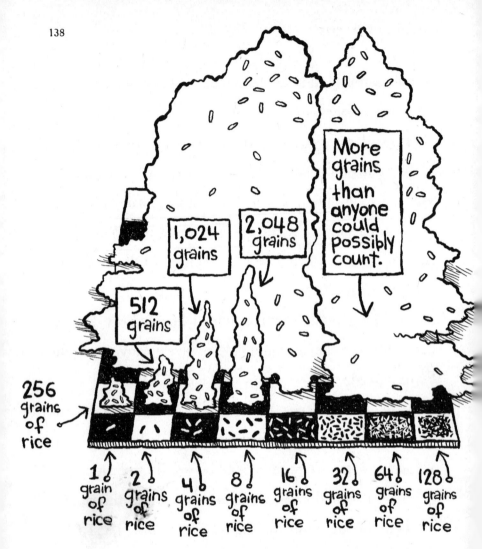

My point is, the hydra was growing new heads at an exponential rate, which was very, very dangerous.

And yet the frightened knights were still lopping its heads off. Each time, two more would grow back.

"Stop cutting off the heads, you dimwits!" Ferkle shouted at them.

No one heard him, of course, because all the heads were roaring so loudly.

I got back to the shore before the other knights. Belinda, Ferkle, Princess Grace, and Rover were piling into a rowboat, ready to set off for the *Herring* and sail away. The chances of that plan working didn't seem very good, as the hydra was bearing down on us quickly and was easily big enough to wade through the harbor to where the *Herring* was anchored and eat it—but then, it was still a better plan than "Stay here and get eaten without even trying to escape."

I jumped into the rowboat, and we began rowing furiously.

"Sorry I couldn't hold off the hydra," I told them. "Let's face it. I'm a terrible knight."

"You really are," Belinda agreed.

Back onshore, the hydra now had thirty-two heads. (Give or take a few. It was very hard to keep count by this point.) The other knights had finally grasped that they shouldn't cut off any more heads and were racing for the remaining rowboats.

Despite my fear that we were about to be devoured by

a thirty-two-headed beast (more or less), I was still hurt by Belinda's words. "Why would you agree with me about being a terrible knight?" I asked. "Is it because I'm not brave?"

"No," Belinda replied. "You're a terrible knight because you think you *have* to be brave. Bravery isn't the most important part of being a knight. In fact, sometimes it doesn't help at all. Like with Sir Cuss. The only plan he ever has is to just run and stab things. And look where that gets him."

She pointed to the shore, where Sir Cuss was whacking several of the hydra's heads with an oar in a desperate attempt to fend it off.

"Then what *is* the most important part of being a knight?" I asked.

"Being *smart*," Belinda replied. "A smart knight knows to not run into danger or do anything rash. Like Sir Eberal. That guy hasn't lived for so long because he stabs everything that comes his way. He's stayed alive by being smart."

"Oh," I said, suddenly feeling very stupid about how I had been behaving throughout the entire voyage.

Then the thought of Sir Eberal reminded me of something he'd said to me.

And all of a sudden I no longer felt stupid.

In fact, I felt quite intelligent.

Because I knew how to defeat the hydra.

CHAPTER FIFTEEN

How We Survived the Hydra

The last thing Sir Eberal had said to me was "More isn't always better."

At the time, that hadn't made much sense.

But now it did.

We had just made it back to the *Herring*. As we climbed aboard, I yelled back to the other knights, "If you want to defeat the hydra, keep cutting the heads off!"

"Are you nuts?" Sir Vyval yelled back. "We've been trying that, and it's only made the situation worse!"

"Because you haven't cut enough off yet!" I hollered. "Keep doing it! Stab like you've never stabbed before!"

By now the other knights were rowing toward the *Herring*, but they weren't going to make it. The hydra

had waded into the harbor, and its heads were about
ready to attack them.

The hydra was about to attack *us* as well. It had plenty of heads to go around. In fact, it had so many heads that some were free to gobble up passing sharks or to snatch seagulls out of the sky. Two were taking a few moments for reflective meditation.

My call to begin stabbing roused the older knights to action once again. They started slicing off heads left and right. *Pop! Pop! Pop! Pop! Pop!*

Meanwhile, Ferkle, Belinda, Princess Grace, and Rover didn't seem so impressed with my plan. So as the angry heads bore down on us, I explained as fast as I could:

"Thehydra'sreallydangerouswithalltheheadsithas*now* buteventuallyitsgoingtohavetoomanyheadsandwhenthat happensitwon'tbeabletofunctionanymorebecauseitwon'tbe abletosupportthemall!"

"Ah!" Ferkle said, looking impressed. "Good thinking, Tim!" Then, as a hydra head tried to swallow him, he took his sword and sliced it off its neck. *Pop!*

Belinda followed his lead and decapitated two incoming heads. *Pop! Pop!*

Princess Grace joined in and cut off some heads too. And so did I. *Pop! Pop! Pop! Pop! Pop!*

Sure enough, each time a head came off, two more grew back. Soon we were surrounded by more hydra heads than we could possibly count. They were gnashing their teeth and eating the sails and gnawing on the masts and making scary faces at whales. The deck of the *Herring* was littered with heads, which were rolling around loose like bowling balls.

But as Sir Eberal had said, more isn't always better. All those heads were cumbersome. ◁ IQ BOOSTER!

("Cumbersome" means "large or heavy and therefore very difficult to use." A large backpack filled with too many books can be cumbersome. Although, in my day, you were much more likely to be carrying a large sack full of rocks.)

The hydra was having more and more trouble supporting all its heads. And coordinating them. Its attacks became less focused and clumsier. Its heads were bonking into one another, and many of its necks were tied in knots.

Meanwhile, all the heads weren't getting along very well. It was as if they had no idea they were even connected to the same animal. Heads were snarling and growling and snapping at one another.

And the whole time we just kept cutting more and more heads off, forcing more and more to grow, until the hydra was ridiculously top heavy.

By this point, its body could no longer support the weight of its many heads. So it toppled over into the harbor and sank to the bottom of the sea.

Normally, when a vicious beast is defeated, everyone is happy, and there is much rejoicing. But we were too exhausted to celebrate. Plus, we were surrounded by loose hydra heads, which was really icky.

Belinda did manage a smile for me, though. "Now *that's* what I was talking about. Being smart is much better than being brave. You figured out how to save us, Tim!"

"Well, Sir Eberal is really the smart one," I said. "He gave us the hint to defeating the hydra."

"He said a couple of cryptic words to us and then ran away," Belinda said dismissively. "For all we know, he was talking about chickens. If he had really wanted to help, he should have said, *Here's how you defeat the hydra.*"

"It still was useful," I said.*

"And now that the hydra is defeated, we can get the mystical amulet of Merryland back," Ferkle announced.

"Oh, that's already taken care of," Princess Grace said. And then she held up the amulet for all of us to see.

We goggled at it in surprise.

---

* Much later, I discovered that Sir Eberal really had been talking about chickens. I was giving him credit he didn't deserve. Turns out, he just didn't like chickens very much.

"How did you get that?" I asked.

"I snuck into the tower while you and the older knights were distracting the hydra," Princess Grace explained. "To be honest, I figured there was a very good chance it was going to eat all of you, so it seemed like the only opportunity to get this back."

"Ooh," Belinda said, impressed. "Looks like Tim isn't the only smart one around here."

Princess Grace beamed. "I also found these other things that Dinkum has stolen from other countries over the years." She held up several very fancy items. "This is the golden crown of Tinkerdink, and the cherished ruby of Fazzini, and the great jewel-encrusted trident of Merland, and the really, really, really expensive necklace of Boobaloo . . ."

"Wow," Belinda said. "The Kingdom of Dinkum is a bunch of jerks. We're going to have to return all that stuff to its rightful owners."

"We're not going *anywhere* for a while," Ferkle pointed out. "Look at our boat."

We did. The *Herring* was in very bad shape after our battle against the hydra. The masts were broken, the sails were torn, our cannons had been eaten, and there were hydra heads all over the place. And we weren't in much better shape. We and the other knights—who had just made it back on the boat—were banged up and worn out.

If any enemies had chosen that moment to attack us, we would have been powerless to defend ourselves.

Which was exactly what happened.

CHAPTER SIXTEEN

What the Deal with That Mysterious Black Ship Was

Just then, the black ship that had been following us all throughout our voyage sailed out from behind the bluffs at the edge of the harbor and fired a warning shot across our bow.

The cannonball screamed over the deck and plunked into the water.

After everything that had happened with the sirens and us nearly sailing off the edge of the world and the people of Dinkum mocking us and the hydra, I had forgotten about the black ship.

But the people aboard the black ship hadn't forgotten about *us*.

Now the ship came up alongside our boat. Its decks

were teeming with pirates. The pirates were aiming weapons at us: cannons, rifles, pistols, crossbows, swords. They all looked very dangerous.

Only two men were not wielding weapons. However, I knew they were possibly the most dangerous people on board.

One was Prince Ruprecht, and the other was his wizard, Nerlim.

Prince Ruprecht and Nerlim did not like me or Belinda

or Ferkle or Princess Grace very much. The last time we had seen them, we had tricked them into getting lost in a labyrinth. (Although, I should point out that they forced us into the labyrinth *first*. And before that, they had plotted to kill us.)

Now they looked very pleased with themselves, because they knew they had us at a disadvantage.

"Hello!" Prince Ruprecht called out. "First, I'd like to thank you for doing all the hard work on this voyage. You defeated Scylla and the hydra so we didn't have to, and showed us how to get past the sirens and that nasty waterfall at the edge of the world! Second, please hand over the Mystical Protective Amulet of Merryland and the other fancy treasure you recovered!"

"Never!" Princess Grace shouted back, glaring at him with intense hatred. "None of these things belong to you!"

Prince Ruprecht laughed at her. "Don't be foolish, Princess! If you don't give those things up, we will blow your ship out of the water!"

"I'd like to see you try!" Princess Grace challenged. "The mystical amulet of Merryland will protect us!"

The moment she said this, Ferkle suddenly grew very worried. "Er, Princess . . . ," he said quietly. "There's something you should know."

Princess Grace ignored him. She held up the amulet defiantly and pronounced, "This amulet has protected Merryland from attack for as long as anyone can remember, and its magical powers will keep us safe now! So go ahead and fire upon us! We will suffer no harm!"

"All right then," Prince Ruprecht said, and pointed to a particularly nasty-looking pirate who was manning a particularly nasty-looking cannon.

The pirate fired the cannon at very close range.

The cannonball blew the entire bow off the *Herring*. After which, our boat began to sink. Quickly.

Apparently the Mystical Protective Amulet of Merryland didn't work.

"I was afraid of that," Ferkle said with a sigh.

The rest of us looked at him in astonishment. "You *knew* it didn't work?" Belinda asked.

"Well, I *suspected* that might be the case," Ferkle said. "A lot of myths turn out to not be true. What matters is whether or not people *believe* them."

"But no one has defeated Merryland for as long as we have had the amulet!" Princess Grace exclaimed.

"Because no one *bothered* to attack Merryland," Ferkle explained. "They thought the amulet would repel them. So, in a sense, the amulet kind of worked—even though, in reality, it didn't. By the way, we should probably get off this boat before we all drown."

As usual, Ferkle was right. The *Herring* was now half underwater.

"No one is getting off that boat until you give me the treasure!" Ruprecht sneered. "Especially the amulet!"

"But the amulet doesn't even work!" I reminded him.

"I know," Ruprecht replied. "But it's still very pretty and shiny and valuable. I want it! So hand it over!"

"No!" Princess Grace told him. "My knights and I would rather die than surrender to a foul wretch like you!"

"Er . . . ," Sir Vyval said uneasily. "That's not quite true." Then he pointed his sword at Princess Grace. "Let's have that treasure."

The other elder knights quickly snatched everything else from Princess Grace's arms.

Princess Grace stared at them in astonishment. "Have you knights been in cahoots ◄IQ BOOSTER! with Ruprecht this entire time?"

(To be "in cahoots" means to be "conspiring secretly," although, to be honest, "cahoot" sounds like the sound a half-crow/half-owl would make.)

"No," said Sir Vyval. "We haven't been in cahoots at all. We only switched sides this very minute."

"I'm not a big fan of drowning," Sir Fass added helpfully.

"Do none of you have any honor?" Princess Grace asked.

"Not really," Sir Cuss said.

Sir Cumference waved the emerald-studded imperial belt of Freedonia above his head so that Ruprecht could see it. "I've got some valuable treasure! Can I come aboard your ship?"

The other knights waved the other treasures they had taken from Princess Grace and asked if they could come aboard as well.

"Certainly!" Prince Ruprecht told them. "All of you are welcome to join my crew!" He then shifted his gaze to Ferkle, Belinda, Princess Grace, Rover, and me and sneered. "Except for the five of you, of course. I've got plans for you troublemakers."

The elder knights quickly scurried across a gangplank from the sinking *Herring* onto Prince Ruprecht's black ship. None of them seemed to feel the slightest bit guilty about this. Not even Sir Mount's horse. Apparently none of them were as brave as I had thought.

"What are your evil plans?" Belinda asked Ruprecht. "Are you going to just leave us on this ship to sink and drown?"

"No," Ruprecht said. "A simple sinking and drowning is too good for the likes of you. Especially after all the trouble you caused me."

"Trouble we caused *you?*" I repeated. "You started this!"

"It took me a very long time to get out of that laby- rinth!" Prince Ruprecht snarled. "And it was very, very scary! And so I vowed revenge upon you. Which I am going to take right now!"

With that, several of his pirates sprang onto our ship and tied us up. Then they took us to the place that had previously been a blank spot on the map, put us in a small boat, and shoved us toward the waterfall at the edge of the world.

Then they sailed away, leaving us hurtling toward our doom.

You have probably noticed that there are not many pages left in this book.

And, therefore, you might be wondering how we are going to rescue ourselves, defeat Prince Ruprecht, recover all the stolen treasures, return them to the kingdoms they came from, and make it home to Merryland in such a short amount of time.

The answer is: we won't.

Instead, this is a cliffhanger. ⟨ IQ BOOSTER !

A "cliffhanger" is the ending of a serial drama that leaves the audience in suspense. So, really, this is good news, because it means there are many more adventures for you to enjoy about me and my friends. However, it is not very good news for me and my friends. We would have been much happier with an easy sail home, followed by a celebratory feast and a good night's sleep.

But that isn't going to happen any time soon. There is much, much more in store for us before we get to . . .

THE END

Acknowledgments

I am extremely much obliged ⟨ IQ BOOSTER! ⟩ to many, many people for their help with this book.

("Obliged" means really, really, really thankful. Without the help of the people I'm going to list below, this book wouldn't exist. Instead, it would be a whole bunch of weird jokes that I'd be annoying my friends with.)

For starters, I'm much obliged to my wonderful illustrator, Stacy Curtis, for bringing my characters and this world to life.

And I'm also much obliged to my incredible team at Simon & Schuster: Krista Vitola, Leila Sales, Justin Chanda, Lucy Ruth Cummins, Kendra Levin, Anne Zafian, Lisa Moraleda, Beth Parker, Jenica Nasworthy, Tom Daly, Chava Wolin, Chrissy Noh, Erin Toller, Brendon MacDonald, Amaris Mang, Christina Pecorale, Victor Iannone, Emily Hutton, Emily Ritter, Michelle Leo, Amy Beaudoin, Nicole Benevento, and Theresa Pang.

Additional obliging goes to my amazing fellow writers (and support group): Sarah Mlynowski, James Ponti, Rose Brock, Julie Buxbaum, Christina Soontornvat, Karina Yan Glaser, Max Brallier, and Gordon Korman.

Even more obliginess goes to my interns, Caroline Curran and Paola Camacho, as well as Megan Vicente; Barry and Carole Patmore; Suz, Darragh, and Ciara Howard; and Ronald and Jane Gibbs.

And finally, I could not be more thankful for my amazing children, Dashiell and Violet, who make me laugh and smile and burst with happiness every day. I love you both more than words can say.

About the Author and Illustrator

Stuart Gibbs is the *New York Times* bestselling author of the Charlie Thorne, FunJungle, Moon Base Alpha, Once Upon a Tim, and Spy School series. He has written screenplays, worked on a whole bunch of animated films, developed TV shows, been a newspaper columnist, and researched capybaras (the world's largest rodents). Stuart lives with his family in Los Angeles. You can learn more about what he's up to at StuartGibbs.com.

Stacy Curtis is a *New York Times* bestselling and award-winning illustrator, cartoonist, and printmaker. He has illustrated more than thirty-five children's books, including *Karate Kakapo*, which won the National Cartoonists Society's Book Illustration award. Stacy lives in the Chicago area with his wife, daughter, and two dogs.